FOURTEEN DAYS

A fine will be charged for each day the book is kept overtime.

SEP 9 1977	DEC 1 5 1984	
OCT 1 1 1977	MAR 1 2 1987	
FEB 1 8 1978	DEC 9 1980	
APR 5 1978	OCT 5	
MAY 6 1978	APR 1 3	
AUG 2 5 1978		
MAR 6 1979 OCT 2 '96		
JUL 1 4 1979		
AUG. 1 7 1979		
DEC. 2 5 1979		
FEB. 1 5 1980		
AUG. 2,5 1980		
NOV. 8 1980		
MAY 6 1983		
JAN. 2 1 1984		
MAY 1 7 1984		
JUN 2 1984		PRINTED IN U.S.A.

GAYLORD 142

Exploring
Space

Kenneth W. Gatland

GROSSET & DUNLAP
A National General Company
Publishers · New York

Managing Editor Chris Milsome
Editorial Assistant Ruth Levenberg
Picture Research Penny Warn
Jacky Newton
Production Stephen Pawley
Design & Research Sarah Tyzack
Projects R. H. Warring
Educational Consultant Tim Bahaire

Series devised by Peter Usborne
Published in the United States by
Grosset & Dunlap Inc.
New York, N.Y.
FIRST PRINTING 1972

contents

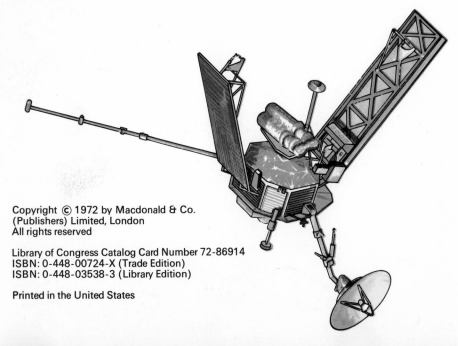

Library of Congress Catalog Card Number 72-86914
ISBN: 0-448-00724-X (Trade Edition)
ISBN: 0-448-03538-3 (Library Edition)

Printed in the United States

The dawn of astronomy

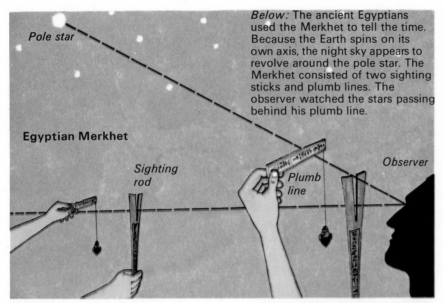

Pole star

Egyptian Merkhet

Sighting rod

Plumb line

Observer

Below: The ancient Egyptians used the Merkhet to tell the time. Because the Earth spins on its own axis, the night sky appears to revolve around the pole star. The Merkhet consisted of two sighting sticks and plumb lines. The observer watched the stars passing behind his plumb line.

The Universe according to Ptolemy

Stars

Planets

Earth

Above: Ptolemy described a "world system" that was first suggested by another Greek, Aristarchus (c. 280 BC). In this system, the Earth was at rest at the center of the Universe. The Moon, Mercury, Venus, Mars, Jupiter, Saturn and the Sun moved around the Earth, and beyond was a fixed sphere of stars.

The first astronomers

Early man gazed at the stars in wonder. He worshipped the Sun and the Moon as gods and built temples in their honor. A solar eclipse, when the Moon passed in front of the Sun, cutting out the sunlight, must have been terrifying. The ancient Chinese imagined the Sun being devoured by a dragon.

For many thousands of years people thought that the Earth was the center of all Creation and that the heavens turned around it once a day.

Calendars and constellations

Early Chinese, Egyptians and Greeks, produced calendars and divided stars into groups, called constellations. Records were kept of such unusual happenings as eclipses. Astronomers in many parts of the world soon began to try to explain what they saw.

A Greek called Aristotle (384–322 BC) showed that the Earth was not flat. Another man, Aristarchus of Samos (c. 280 BC), even suggested that the Earth moved around the Sun. As there was no evidence to support this theory, many people did not agree with him.

Up until the seventeenth century astronomers' observations were made only with the naked eye. They were limited to measuring the apparent positions of the stars and planets which were seen merely as points of light. It took the invention of the telescope to convince man that his world was not the center of the Universe.

Above: Ptolemy of Alexandria (c. AD 120–180) was a Greek scientist who studied mathematics, astronomy and geography.

16th century astrolabe

Above: The astrolabe was used to measure the altitude of stars and planets. From this, time and latitude could be calculated. The astrolabe is believed to have been invented by the Greek, Hipparchus (c. 160–125 BC).

Left: Edmund Gunter (1581–1626), the English mathematician, invented several measuring instruments including the quadrant. It was used to measure the altitude of the Sun in degrees, in order to find the hour of the day.

The telescope breakthrough in astronomy

Above: **Galileo Galilei (1564–1642)** used the newly invented telescope to observe stars and planets.

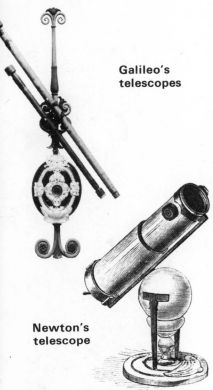

Galileo's telescopes

Newton's telescope

Galileo shows the way

When Galileo (1564–1642) looked at the planets for the first time through a telescope, he must have been startled to see, not points of light in the heavens, but rounded globes. In rapid succession, he discovered craters and mountains on the Moon, the phases of Venus, spots on the Sun, and the four bright moons of Jupiter.

Beginning in 1609, Galileo was the first man to view the heavens through a telescope. His observations of stars and planets demonstrated the truth of Copernicus's theory that the Sun, and not the Earth, was at the center of our solar system. The telescope Galileo used was not the first. A Dutch spectacle-maker called Hans Lippershey probably made the first telescope.

Newton and the reflector

Sir Isaac Newton (1642–1727) contributed much to astronomy, including the invention of the reflecting telescope.

Thanks to these and other great pioneers of science, telescopes have enormously enlarged our knowledge of the surrounding universe. Until recently the world's largest telescope was the Hale reflector on Mount Palomar in California. Its 200 in. (5.08 m.) mirror weighs 17 tons (817 kg.). Now the Russians have built an even bigger reflector telescope on Mount Semirodniki, 6,800 ft. (2,070 m.) in the Northern Caucasus in the USSR. This has a 236 in. (6 m.) mirror. Astronomers do not look through this type of telescope. They use it to photograph the heavens and to analyze the light from remote objects such as stars, and from vast clusters of stars called galaxies.

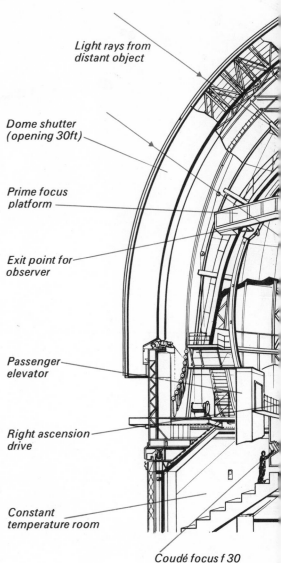

Light rays from distant object

Dome shutter (opening 30ft)

Prime focus platform

Exit point for observer

Passenger elevator

Right ascension drive

Constant temperature room

Coudé focus f 30

Above: Two telescopes, used by Galileo in 1609–10, mounted for exhibition. The larger instrument magnified up to 20 times. Galileo made his first telescope by mounting a convex and a concave lens in a lead tube. This was a simple refractor telescope *(see diagram right)*. It suffered blurring and rainbow effects around the edges.
Above: Fifty-nine years later, Newton's reflecting telescope overcame these defects by replacing the object lens with a concave mirror.

Principles of the telescope

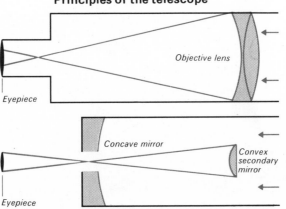

Objective lens

Eyepiece

Concave mirror

Convex secondary mirror

Eyepiece

Left: **The refractor**
The simplest telescope is the *refractor*. The objective lens forms a small image which is observed through the magnifying eyepiece. The same principle is used in binoculars and opera glasses.

Left: **The reflector**
Most serious astronomy depends on *reflector* telescopes. The diagram shows the Cassegrain type. A small image formed by the concave mirror is reflected from the convex mirror and observed through a hole in the concave mirror.

The Hale 200in reflector

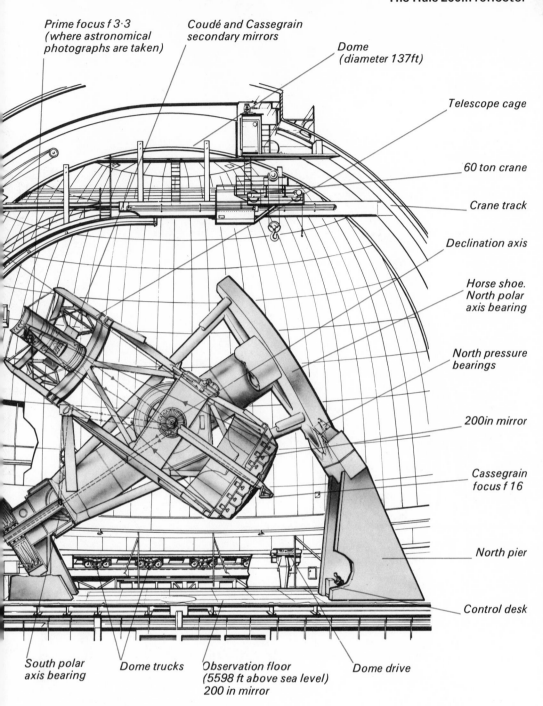

Prime focus f 3·3 (where astronomical photographs are taken)

Coudé and Cassegrain secondary mirrors

Dome (diameter 137ft)

Telescope cage

60 ton crane

Crane track

Declination axis

Horse shoe. North polar axis bearing

North pressure bearings

200in mirror

Cassegrain focus f 16

North pier

Control desk

South polar axis bearing

Dome trucks

Observation floor (5598 ft above sea level) 200 in mirror

Dome drive

Hale Observatory, Mount Palomar

Above: The Hale 200 in. (508 cm.) reflector is at Mount Palomar, California. Large telescopes of this kind, which are moved by motors to follow the stars, must be set in heavy mountings to avoid vibration. The observer's cage allows photographs to be taken at the prime focus. Two additional systems, Cassegrain and Coudé, can also be used. In the Cassegrain system light is reflected to a fixed point beyond the main mirror through a special opening. In the Coudé, light is reflected to a fixed point outside the telescope.

Left: Mount Palomar Observatory.

Skylab observatory in space

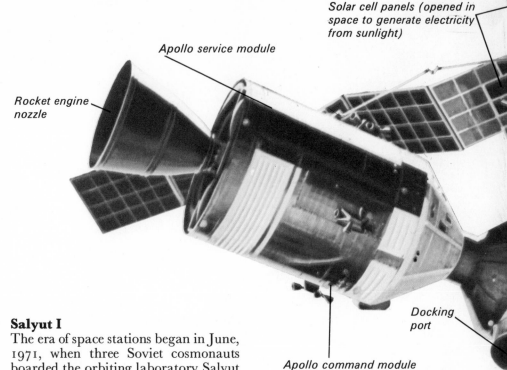

Solar cell panels (opened in space to generate electricity from sunlight)

Apollo service module

Rocket engine nozzle

Docking port

Apollo command module

Skylab mission profile

Flight 1

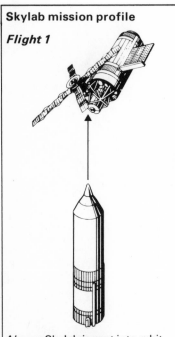

Above: Skylab is sent into orbit, unmanned, by the first two stages of a Saturn V. A day later, three men in a module are launched to dock with it for a period of 28 days. Two replacement crews are flown up to the station to continue experiments at intervals of 80 days. Each crew remains in space for up to 56 days.

Flight 2

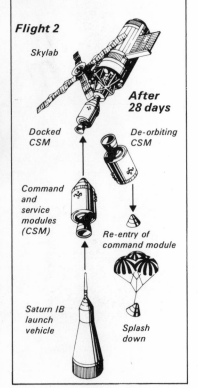

Skylab

After 28 days

Docked CSM

De-orbiting CSM

Command and service modules (CSM)

Re-entry of command module

Saturn IB launch vehicle

Splash down

Salyut I

The era of space stations began in June, 1971, when three Soviet cosmonauts boarded the orbiting laboratory Salyut 1 in Earth-orbit. Although the flight ended tragically with their deaths, it marked a major breakthrough in astronomy today. These spacecraft can be used as observatories. From them, it is possible to observe much more of the Universe than from within the Earth's atmosphere. They can detect radiation that does not penetrate the atmosphere.

America's orbital workshop

America's Skylab is more than three times the weight of the Soviet station.

It is made from the third (S-IVB) stage of the Saturn V rocket which sent men to the Moon. The rocket's hydrogen fuel tank has been made into two-story accommodations for three astronauts. They have as much room as in an average-sized house. Experiments include detailed observation of the Sun with the Apollo Telescope Mount (ATM), and a study of natural resources on Earth.

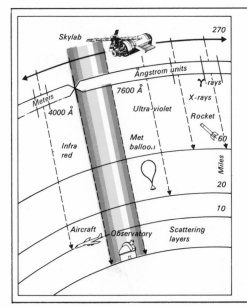

Skylab

270

Ångstrom units

7600 Å

γ-rays

X-rays

Meters

4000 Å

Ultra-violet

Rocket

Infra red

Met balloon

60

Miles

20

10

Aircraft

Observatory

Scattering layers

Left: **Widening the spectrum**
Our knowledge of the surrounding Universe arrives in the form of radiation from distant stars and galaxies. Radiation is energy traveling in waves. The wavelengths are measured in Å (Ångstroms) named after the Swedish physicist Anders Ångstrom. The radiation between 4000 Å and 7600 Å is called light and is visible to the human eye. Radiation of shorter and longer wavelength can only be "observed" using special instruments.

Most of the range, or spectrum, of radiation is cut off from ground observers by scattering and absorption in the Earth's atmosphere. The dotted areas on the diagram show the extent to which various radiations are cut off.

The heights to which airplanes, balloons and small sounding rockets can ascend are also shown. The space station is the only instrument to "observe" the whole spectrum.

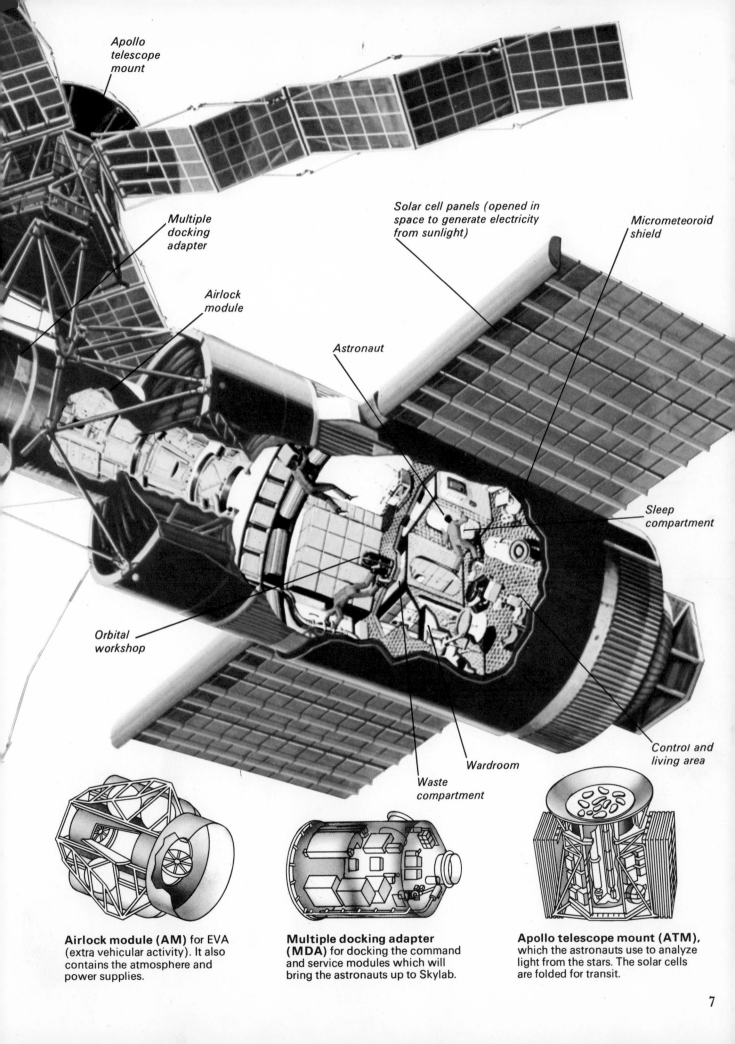

Apollo telescope mount

Multiple docking adapter

Airlock module

Solar cell panels (opened in space to generate electricity from sunlight)

Micrometeoroid shield

Astronaut

Sleep compartment

Orbital workshop

Control and living area

Wardroom

Waste compartment

Airlock module (AM) for EVA (extra vehicular activity). It also contains the atmosphere and power supplies.

Multiple docking adapter (MDA) for docking the command and service modules which will bring the astronauts up to Skylab.

Apollo telescope mount (ATM), which the astronauts use to analyze light from the stars. The solar cells are folded for transit.

The Solar System family of the Sun

Nicolaus Copernicus (1473-1543)

Above: Copernicus, a Polish astronomer, was the founder of the Sun-centered theory of the Universe. He also calculated that the Earth revolved once every 24 hours.

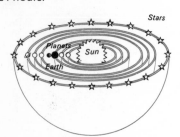

The Universe according to Copernicus

The nine planets

The Earth on which we live is part of the Solar System of nine planets which travel around the Sun. In order of distance they are Mercury, Venus, Earth, Mars, Jupiter, Saturn, Uranus, Neptune and Pluto. Between Mars and Jupiter are the asteroids, a belt of rocky debris which may be the remains of a tenth planet, or one that failed to form.

The planets follow elliptical paths (an ellipse is like a squashed circle) so that their distances from the Sun are constantly changing. Some have moons revolving around them which they take with them on their immense journeys.

Nearest the Sun, Mercury orbits with an average speed of 107,000 m p.h.; at the farthest distance, Pluto creeps along at 10,600 m.p.h.

The force of gravity

The invisible force that binds the planets to the Sun and the moons to the planets is gravitation. This is the force of attraction between bodies. Its strength depends upon how much matter the bodies contain (their mass) and how far apart they are. If, by some magic,

gravitation was suddenly cut off, the planets and their moons would fly off into space.

Stars and galaxies

Planets and moons have no light of their own. They can be seen only because they reflect light from the Sun. The Sun itself is one of millions of stars bound together in an immense spiral structure which also contains gas and dust. This spiral is called the Galaxy. Beyond it are countless other galaxies of stars. It is most unlikely that ours is the only solar system. Many other stars probably have their own families of circling planets.

Orbits of the planets
(drawn to scale)

In April, 1972, a group of astronomers suggested that another planet may yet be discovered far beyond the orbit of Pluto. They based their judgement on the gravitational effects the unseen body appeared to have on Halley's and other comets.

Key
A Diameter
B Average distance from Sun.
C Turns on axis in
D Moves around Sun in

Pluto
A 3,700 miles
B 3,666 million miles
C 6 days 9 hours
D 247·7 years

Neptune
A 31,200 miles
B 2,793 million miles
C 14 hours
D 164·79 years

Uranus
A 29,300 miles
B 1,783 million miles
C 10 hours 48 mins.
D 84·01 years

Saturn
A 75,100 miles
B 886·1 million miles
C 10 hours 14 mins.
D 29·46 years

Right: **The great work of Tycho Brahe**
Early astronomers who insisted that the Earth was not the center of the Universe were accused of contradicting the teaching of the Church. One who tried to bridge the gap between the Copernican theory of a central Sun and the deeply held religious beliefs was the Danish nobleman Tycho Brahe. He agreed that the planets moved around the Sun but held that the Sun must itself be in orbit around the Earth.

Though he had made his observations before the invention of the telescope, he produced the most detailed star catalogue and recorded the supernova (star explosion) of 1572.

Most important of all, Tycho Brahe's results were used by his former assistant Johannes Kepler (1571–1630). He proved that all the known planets, the Earth included, moved around the Sun in elliptical, and not precisely circular, paths.

How planets form
As a new star condenses from gas and dust, it spins and develops a magnetic field. The magnetic field controls the distribution of a lens-shaped disc of residual material from which planets and other bodies form by accretion. As they continue to circle the new-born star, they sweep up "loose" material by gravitation, becoming more concentrated until solid cores are formed.
The planets move in elliptical paths around the Sun. An ellipse can be drawn very simply. Stick two pins in a board and make a loop of string. Use the string to guide a pencil.

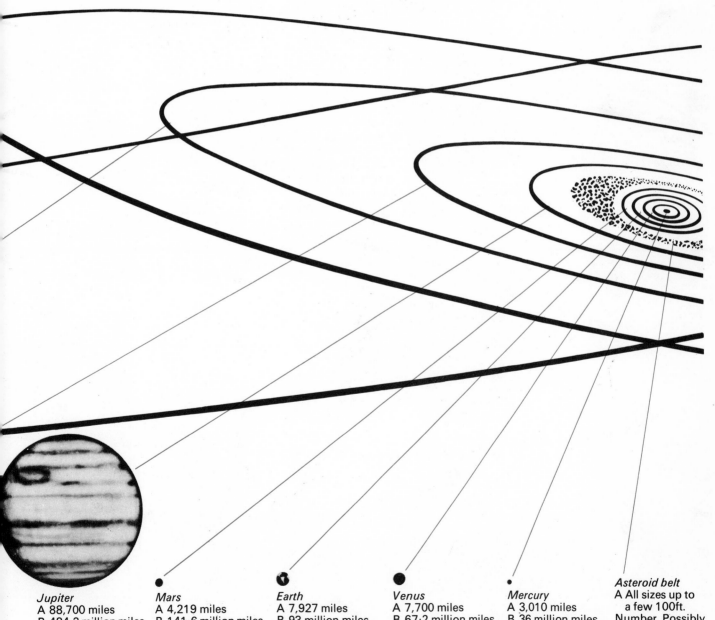

Jupiter
A 88,700 miles
B 484·3 million miles
C 9 hours 51 mins.
D 11·86 years

Mars
A 4,219 miles
B 141·6 million miles
C 24 hours 37 mins.
D 686·98 days

Earth
A 7,927 miles
B 93 million miles
C 23 hours 56 mins.
D 365·257 days

Venus
A 7,700 miles
B 67·2 million miles
C 243 days
D 224·7 days

Mercury
A 3,010 miles
B 36 million miles
C 58 days 12 hours
D 87·9 days

Asteroid belt
A All sizes up to a few 100ft.
Number. Possibly as many as 100,000

A star called the Sun

The life-giving furnace

The Sun is a star around which revolve nine major planets, 32 moons, scores of comets, thousands of asteroids (minor planets) and millions of meteoroids. It is an immense body of highly condensed gas, with a diameter of about 864,000 miles. It weighs about 330,000 times as much as the Earth.

The Sun is believed to have formed from gas and dust over 5,000 million years ago. As gas built up, the core became highly compressed, temperatures rose, and hydrogen atoms were converted into helium according to the principles of thermonuclear reaction. At the core of the "solar furnace" temperatures may well exceed 15,000,000°C. The surface temperature is about 6,000°C.

Ocean of fire

The part of the Sun we actually see is called the photosphere. The turbulent region of hot gases next to the surface is the chromosphere, and extending from that are the transparent gases of the corona. Flowing away from the corona is the solar wind of charged particles which surrounds the Earth and distorts its magnetic field.

Sun worship in Ancient Egypt

Above: A mural of the Ancient Egyptian god Hathor holding the Sun. It was believed that gods escorted the Sun across the sky during the day. At night they traveled together through the underworld.

Right: The surface layer of the Sun is called the *photosphere.* The light we normally see shines from it. *Sunspots* appear from time to time. They are usually in pairs or in large clusters *(circle inset right).* The darker region of a sunspot, the *umbra,* is surrounded by a less dark region, the *penumbra.*

Right: Solar prominences are connected with sunspot activity. These prominences are great arches of glowing gases which follow magnetic lines of force. They erupt from the surface and fall back. Prominences can leap thousands of miles.

The three pictures of a solar prominence *(right)* were photographed at Johannesburg Observatory, South Africa, on March 24, 1953. A brilliant tongue of gas burst high above the Sun's surface. The time interval between the first and last photograph was 12 minutes.

A WARNING. NEVER look at the Sun through a telescope or binoculars. This can cause blindness.

The photosphere

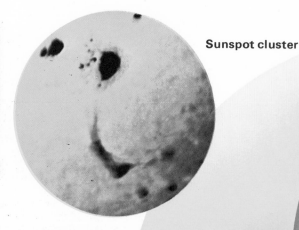

Sunspot cluster

Solar prominence

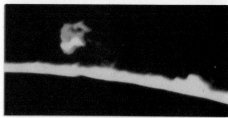

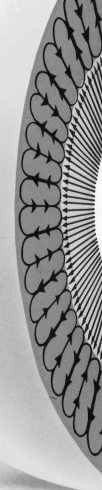

Sunspots and prominences

Every 11.1 years the Sun undergoes a period of maximum sunspot activity. Spots occur mainly in pairs in well-defined belts and can reach diameters of tens of thousands of miles. They are probably caused by magnetic disturbances in the Sun's surface which distort the upward flow of hot gases. "Cool" areas of about 4,000°C are produced which appear darker than their surroundings. Bright patches accompany spots and brilliant flares erupt in active regions, spraying atomic particles into space.

Charged particles from the Sun, particularly those emitted by solar flares, cause radio fade-out, magnetic storms and brilliant auroral displays such as the Northern Lights.

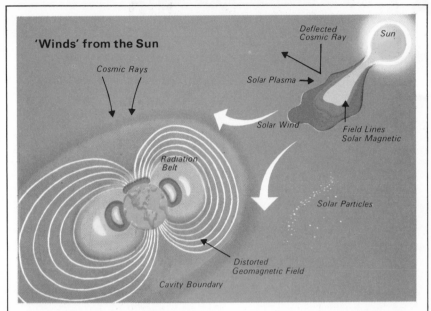

'Winds' from the Sun

Cosmic Rays

Deflected Cosmic Ray

Sun

Solar Plasma

Solar Wind

Field Lines Solar Magnetic

Radiation Belt

Solar Particles

Distorted Geomagnetic Field

Cavity Boundary

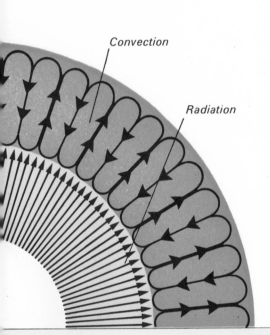

Convection

Radiation

The corona during an eclipse

Above: The *corona* is a pearly-white halo around the Sun made up of gases that are highly rarefied (thinly spread out). It can be seen clearly during a solar eclipse.

The corona is so thin that even the most fragile comets can pass through it without any change to their motion. Sometimes, the clearly defined halo extends outwards to over 15 million miles from the Sun.

Above: Apart from violent flares, the Sun also sends out constant streams of slower-moving particles. They flow in streams called solar winds. The Earth's magnetic field acts as a buffer to these winds, trapping them in belts.

Below: The Earth's radiation belts were discovered by Dr. J. A. Van Allen.

How the Sun works—the thermonuclear reaction

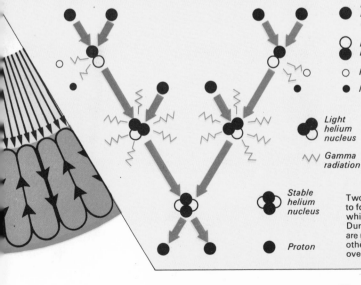

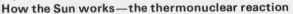

● Hydrogen nucleus (Proton)

◉ Deuterium nucleus

○ Positron

● Neutrino

Light helium nucleus

〰 Gamma radiation

Stable helium nucleus

● Proton

Two protons collide and fuse together to form a nucleus of deuterium, which has one proton and one neutron. During this fusion two particles, called a positron and a neutrino, fly out.

The nucleus of deuterium captures another hydrogen nucleus, or proton, forming the nucleus of light helium, which has two protons and one neutron. Powerful gamma rays are given off during this fusion process.

Two light helium nuclei will join together to form an ordinary helium nucleus, which has two neutrons and two protons. During this stage the two spare protons are released. They fly out to collide with other protons and start the whole process over again.

Left: In the center of the Sun, pressure and temperature are enormous. Particles of atoms dash around so fast that collisions occur.

One type of particle is the proton, which is the nucleus of a hydrogen atom that has lost its only electron. Normally electrical forces of repulsion keep positively charged protons apart (just as the like poles of two magnets are repelled). But under great pressure, as in the Sun, these forces are overcome and protons collide. The protons fuse together and form nuclei of helium.

During the process, which takes place in several stages, energy is released as radiation. The diagram shows the three probable main stages of the process.

The great space race

Helium pressurizing bottles
S-11/S-1VB stage separation
Pitch-control motor
Solid propel
launch esc
motor

How a rocket engine works

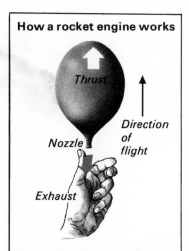

Above: The hot exhaust gases escaping from the rocket nozzle at high speed produce a reaction in the opposite direction—a forward thrust. The same principle applies when you blow up a balloon and release it. As air rushes out, the balloon shoots off in the opposite direction.

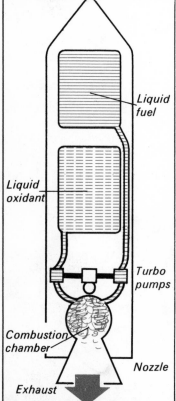

Above: Most rocket engines use liquid fuels which are fed from separate tanks and burned in a combustion chamber. A typical propellant mixture, used in the first stage of Saturn V, is kerosene and liquid oxygen.

Development of the rocket

Before man could investigate the Moon and the planets at first hand, powerful rockets had to be developed which could "break the chains" of Earth's gravity. For a rocket to escape from the Earth's pull, it must reach a speed of more than 6.95 miles per second. Konstantin Tsiolkovsky, a Russian teacher, worked out the mathematics of space flight at the beginning of the twentieth century.

But it was Dr. Robert H. Goddard who launched the world's first liquid-propellant rocket in 1926.

The V-2 rocket, developed by the Germans under Dr. Wernher von Braun during World War II, was a huge technical advance. It weighed 12½ tons, reached a top speed of 3,500 m.p.h., and could carry a one-ton warhead a distance of nearly 200 miles. More than 1,000 were fired against London and southeast England from sites on the Continent in 1944–45.

After the war, Dr. von Braun worked on rockets for the U.S. Army. One of them—Juno 1, a development of the Jupiter C—placed the U.S. first satellite into Earth-orbit on February 1, 1958, at a speed of nearly 18,000 m.p.h.

The space race

The world's first artificial satellite, Sputnik 1, had already been placed into orbit by the Russians on October 4, 1957. The same type of rocket—a big liquid propellant inter-continental ballistic missile (ICBM) fitted with a new top stage—gave Russia her second major triumph. On April 12, 1961, Yuri Gagarin became the first man to go into orbit. Valentina Tereshkova became the first space woman in 1963.

The space race now began in earnest. On February 20, 1962, the United States put her first spaceman, Col. John Glenn, into orbit in a Mercury capsule launched by an Atlas ICBM. Russia followed with the two/three man Voskhod spacecraft and made the first space walk.

The United States replied with the big Titan 2 ICBM which launched a series of Gemini spacecraft into Earth-orbit, eventually achieving the first rendezvous and docking between two orbiting spacecraft. This paved the way for the Apollo man-on-the-Moon program.

Liquid oxygen tank
Gimbal mour
Ullage motor

Five J-2 engines 225,000 lb thrust each

Reaching for the Moon

Manned Moon landings required a huge launch vehicle weighing over 3,000 tons at lift-off. The three-stage Saturn V stands 363 ft. tall—60 ft. taller than the Statue of Liberty on its column!

Although the Russians also practiced space docking in Earth-orbit with Soyuz vehicles, no Russian manned Moon rocket appeared. The first men to step onto the Moon's ancient dust were Apollo astronauts Neil Armstrong and Edwin Aldrin. The date was July 21, 1969.

Firsts in space

Konstantin Tsiolkovsky produced the first mathematical treatise on space travel in 1903.

Robert H. Goddard launched the world's first liquid-propellant rocket in 1926. The Americans were thus first to experiment.

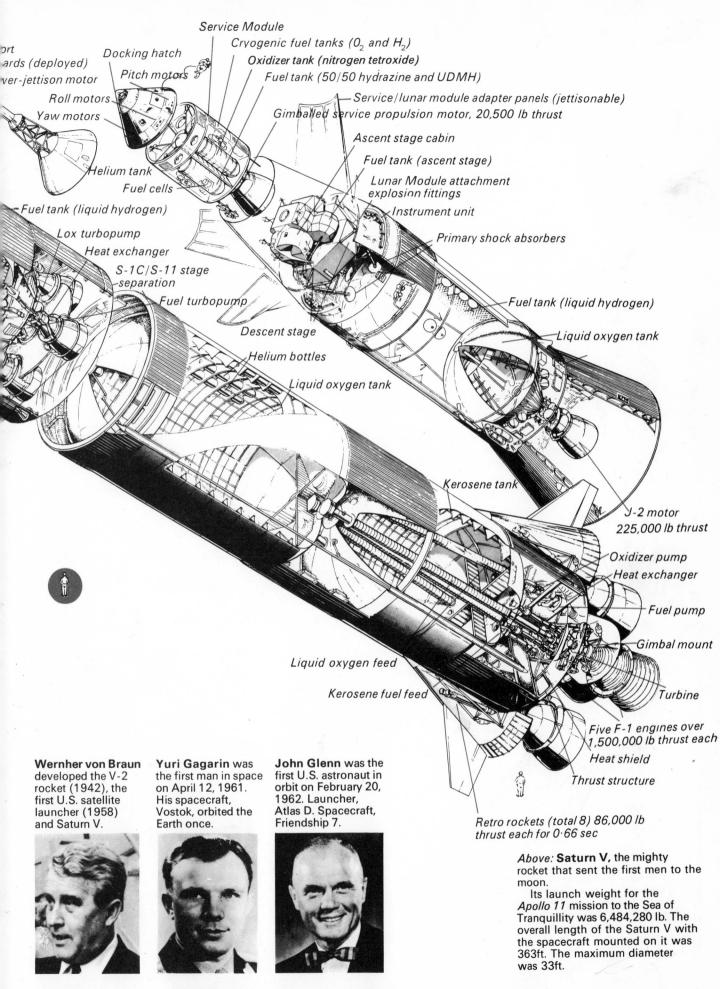

port
ards (deployed)
ver-jettison motor
Roll motors
Yaw motors

Docking hatch
Pitch motors

Service Module
Cryogenic fuel tanks (O_2 and H_2)
Oxidizer tank (nitrogen tetroxide)
Fuel tank (50/50 hydrazine and UDMH)
Service/lunar module adapter panels (jettisonable)
Gimballed service propulsion motor, 20,500 lb thrust

Helium tank
Fuel cells

Ascent stage cabin
Fuel tank (ascent stage)
Lunar Module attachment
explosion fittings
Instrument unit

Fuel tank (liquid hydrogen)
Lox turbopump
Heat exchanger
S-1C/S-11 stage
separation
Fuel turbopump

Primary shock absorbers

Descent stage
Helium bottles
Liquid oxygen tank

Fuel tank (liquid hydrogen)

Liquid oxygen tank

Kerosene tank

J-2 motor
225,000 lb thrust

Oxidizer pump
Heat exchanger

Fuel pump

Gimbal mount

Liquid oxygen feed

Kerosene fuel feed

Turbine

Five F-1 engines over
1,500,000 lb thrust each
Heat shield
Thrust structure

Retro rockets (total 8) 86,000 lb
thrust each for 0·66 sec

Wernher von Braun
developed the V-2
rocket (1942), the
first U.S. satellite
launcher (1958)
and Saturn V.

Yuri Gagarin was
the first man in space
on April 12, 1961.
His spacecraft,
Vostok, orbited the
Earth once.

John Glenn was the
first U.S. astronaut in
orbit on February 20,
1962. Launcher,
Atlas D. Spacecraft,
Friendship 7.

Above: **Saturn V,** the mighty
rocket that sent the first men to the
moon.
  Its launch weight for the
Apollo 11 mission to the Sea of
Tranquillity was 6,484,280 lb. The
overall length of the Saturn V with
the spacecraft mounted on it was
363ft. The maximum diameter
was 33ft.

First stop—the Moon

Several important questions had to be answered before man could land on the Moon. Some people thought the crust would not bear the weight of a spaceship. Others supposed the vehicle might sink in moondust. There was widespread concern that craters and boulders would prevent a safe landing.

To discover the truth, a number of unmanned spacecraft were sent ahead as pathfinders.

Luna 2

First to hit the Moon was Russia's *Luna 2* in September 1959 *(above)*. During its 33½ hour flight, instruments measured conditions in space, but the probe's magnetometer found no evidence that the Moon possessed a magnetic field.

It was more than five years before instruments were landed in working order. *Luna 9 (below)* televised pictures of its landing site in the Ocean of Storms in January 1966.

Surveyor 3

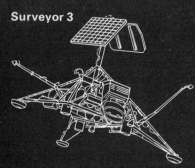

The United States followed in June, 1966, by soft-landing the three-legged *Surveyor 1* in the Ocean of Storms. It sent back 11,150 pictures. More landings followed at different points. *Luna 13* photographed its landing site and analyzed the lunar soil with an instrument which reported back by radio. *Surveyor 3*, besides sending 6,320 pictures from the Ocean of Storms, used a mechanical scoop to examine moonsoil under remote control from a station in California.

Three more *Surveyor* space probes were launched before the US attempted a manned landing.

Man on the Moon

Before a world audience, linked by television, the first men on the Moon practiced walking and jumping under a sixth of Earth gravity.

Astronauts Neil Armstrong and Edwin Aldrin landed their *Apollo 11* mooncraft in the Sea of Tranquillity on July 20, 1969. When they emerged they found the soil was a brownish, medium grey, slightly cohesive, granular material which contained tiny glass beads.

Apollo 11 rock specimen

They collected about 44 lb. (20 kg.) of moonsoil and rocks.

The thin section of moon rock *(above)* is highly magnified. The colors are caused by the interaction of polarized light with the crystalline structure of various minerals. The sample contains a variety of minerals, including ilmenite which is a valuable source of oxygen.

The oldest rocks picked up by the *Apollo 11* astronauts were probably formed 3,500 million years ago

Fern growing in moonsoil

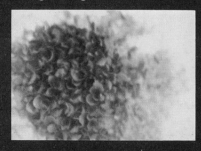

when there was violent volcanic activity and huge meteorites struck the Moon. The glass beads in the moonsoil are thought to have been produced by impact shocks.

Later moon expeditions found similar conditions with local variations. The lunar rock *(below)* is from the *Apollo 12* mission to the Ocean of Storms. It shows vesicles, or cavities, formed by the expansion of vapor in a molten mass.

The rocks were analyzed by world scientists. Three quarters of the rocks were brecchias—compressed dust and fragments solidified by heat. Others were igneous—they were once in a molten state. Compared with similar Earth rocks they had far more elements with

Apollo 12 rock specimen

high melting points such as chromium, titanium, yttrium and zirconium.

While Apollo astronauts explored the surface, the third crew member of the expedition remained orbiting the Moon in the Apollo command ship making detailed observations. A spectacular view *(below)* of the crater Eratosthenes was obtained from *Apollo 12*.

Crater Eratosthenes

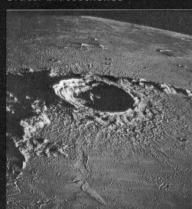

Left: Certain Earth plants such as ferns seemed to thrive when grown in moonsoil under laboratory conditions. Yet scientists did not detect water or life, past or present, in any of the early samples taken from the Moon.

Aristarchus

Ocean of Storms

Gassend

The Moon—nearside

Sea of Cold

Dew Jura Mts. Plato Alpine Valley Aristoteles

Bay of Rainbows Alps Caucasus Mts. Lake of Dreams

●L17
Sea of Rains

Archimedes

Marsh of Sleep

●A15 Sea of Serenity ●A17

Eratosthenes Haemus Mts. Sea of Crises

Apennine Mts.

Copernicus Sea of Vapours

Reinhold Seething Bay Sea of Tranquillity

●A12 ●A14 Central Bay ●A11 ●L 20

Fra Mauro Hipparchus L 16

Ptolemaeus ●A16 Foaming Sea

Alb'ategnius Theophilus Sea of Fertility

Alphonsus ●A16 Sea of Nectar

Sea of Clouds ●A17 Pyrenees Mts.

Altai Scarp Langrenus

of Moisture

Stofler Maurolycus

Tycho Janssen

ickard Longmontanus Maginus

Schiller Clavius

Above: The Moon always turns the same face to the Earth. The U.S. and the USSR have spent over a decade exploring it by means of space probes. The first probes were destroyed as they hit the Moon. In 1966 the USSR made the first soft landing with working instruments. Three years later the U.S. put the first men on the Moon.

Right: No one knew what the far side of the Moon was like until Luna 3 was sent around it in 1959. Pictures taken by the space probe were sent back to Earth by television. The first maps of the far side were made from these pictures and also from photographs sent back by other spacecraft.

The Moon—farside

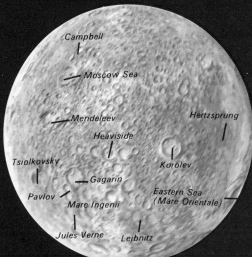

Campbell

Moscow Sea

Mendeleev Hertzsprung

Heaviside

Tsiolkovsky Korolev

Gagarin

Pavlov Eastern Sea
(Mare Orientale)
Mare Ingenii

Jules Verne Leibnitz

Key to Moon Map.

●**A11** **Apollo 11.** Man's first landing on the Moon, Sea of Tranquillity, July 20, 1969, by Neil Armstrong and Edwin Aldrin in *Eagle* Lunar Module. Astronauts set out scientific instruments and collected some 44 lb. of rock and soil samples. Total stay time, 21 hr. 36 min.

●**A12** **Apollo 12.** Landing in Ocean of Storms, November 19, 1969, by Charles Conrad and Alan Bean in *Intrepid* Lunar Module. Astronauts set out ALSEP research station and collected 74.9 lb. of rock and soil samples; also parts from Surveyor 3 moon probe. Total stay time, 31 hr. 31 min.

●**L16** **Luna 16.** First successful soft-landing, Sea of Fertility, September 20, 1970, by robot moon probe capable of extracting core sample under remote control and bringing it to Earth. Return sample weighed under 4 oz. (about 100 grams). Total stay time, 26 hr. 25 min.

●**L17** **Luna 17.** First successful soft-landing, Sea of Rains, November 17, 1970, of remote-controlled roving vehicle, Lunokhod 1, reporting to Earth by radio. Covered total distance of 34,588 ft. (10,542 m.) between November 17, 1970 and October 4, 1971.

●**A14** **Apollo 14.** Landing in Fra Mauro region, February 5, 1971, by Alan Shepard and Edgar Mitchell in Lunar Module *Antares*. Astronauts set out research station and collected about 98 lb. of rock and soil samples. Total stay time, 33 hr. 31 min.

●**A15** **Apollo 15.** Landing in Hadley-Apennine region, July 30, 1971, by David Scott and James Irwin in Lunar Module *Falcon*. First use of *Lunar Roving Vehicle (LRV)*. Astronauts set out research station and collected about 173 lb. of rock and soil samples. Total stay time, 66 hr. 55 min.

●**L20** **Luna 20.** Second successful soft-landing, mountainous area between Sea of Fertility and Sea of Crisis, February 21, 1972, by robot vehicle capable of extracting core sample. Returned sample weighed about 4 oz. (100 grams). Total stay time, 25 hr. 39 min.

●**A16** **Apollo 16.** Landing, in Descartes region, April 16, 1972, by John Young and Charles Duke.

●**A17** **Apollo 17.** Last scheduled U.S. manned landing, in Taurus-Littrow region, December, 1972, by Eugene Cernan and Dr. Harrison Schmitt (geologist).

N.B. Apollo 13 mission—to Fra Mauro—in April, 1970, abandoned some 205,000 miles short of Moon. Astronauts returned safely.

Explorers on wheels

Russia landed the first self-propelled moon-car, Lunokhod 1, on November 17, 1970, in the Sea of Rains.

Despite its robot nature, Lunokhod 1 carried out a number of important experiments sending the results to Earth automatically on command.

At stopping points, instruments examined the moonsoil's mechanical properties and chemical composition. An X-ray telescope scanned the heavens, and laser signals sent from Earth were reflected back from the vehicle to measure the Earth-Moon distance. Laser signals also measured the Moon's libration (rocking motion) and variations in the Earth's axial spin. During each successive lunar night, lasting nearly 14 Earth days, Lunokhod was "rested" with its solar cell panel closed to conserve heat.

Man versus machines

Though man will never be entirely replaced in space exploration, robot vehicles have an important part to play. The reasoning ability of the human brain is unmatched by any machine, yet for certain tasks robots are cheaper and no less effective. Special instruments allow the robot to see, touch, and listen, and what it finds can be recorded and sent to Earth in the form of radio signals.

Robots need never return

The robot is cheaper, largely because of the astronaut's need to be enveloped by a replica of Earth's atmosphere, in the shape of a pressure cabin or pressure suit at each stage of his mission. Human explorers also need to be returned to Earth. This makes a great deal of difference to the weight, size and power of space vehicles.

If it breaks down, the robot can be abandoned without loss of life. It can also be sent into places where it would be dangerous for men to go, such as deep craters or crevasses on the Moon.

Russia landed Lunokhod 1, the first self-propelled mooncar, on the Sea of Rains on November 17, 1970.

Russia has begun to make advances with robot spacecraft which land on the Moon, drill into the soil and return samples to Earth. In September, 1970, *Luna 16* landed in the Sea of Fertility. An under 4 oz. (100 gram) core sample was extracted by a hollow drill and sealed in a capsule. It was rocketed back and landed by parachute in the Soviet Union. In February, 1972, *Luna 20* obtained a core sample from a mountainous region between the Sea of Fertility and the Sea of Crises.

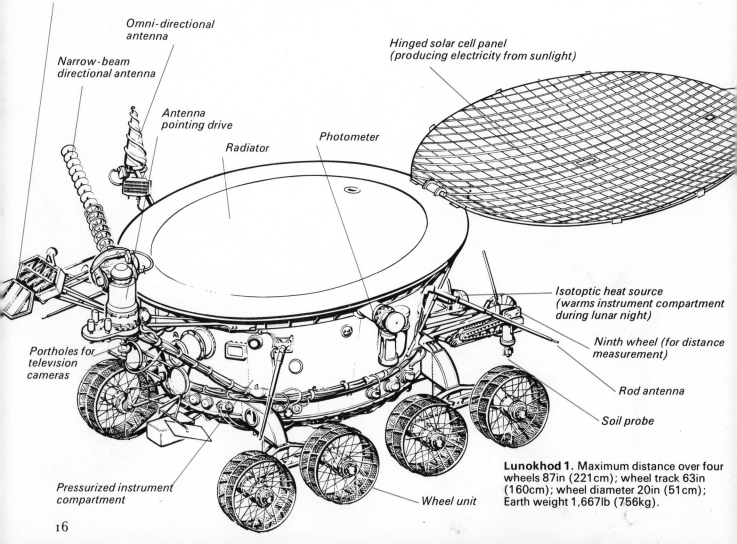

French-built laser reflector (for checking Earth-Moon distances, etc.)

Omni-directional antenna

Narrow-beam directional antenna

Antenna pointing drive

Radiator

Photometer

Hinged solar cell panel (producing electricity from sunlight)

Isotoptic heat source (warms instrument compartment during lunar night)

Ninth wheel (for distance measurement)

Rod antenna

Soil probe

Portholes for television cameras

Pressurized instrument compartment

Wheel unit

Lunokhod 1. Maximum distance over four wheels 87in (221cm); wheel track 63in (160cm); wheel diameter 20in (51cm); Earth weight 1,667lb (756kg).

High-gain (long range) antenna

Lunar Roving Vehicle (LRV)

Above: Apollo 15 astronauts with the *LRV* exploring the Hadley Rille.

Low-gain (short range) antenna

16 mm. camera

TV camera

Display console (Instrument panel)

Hand controller

Lunar drill

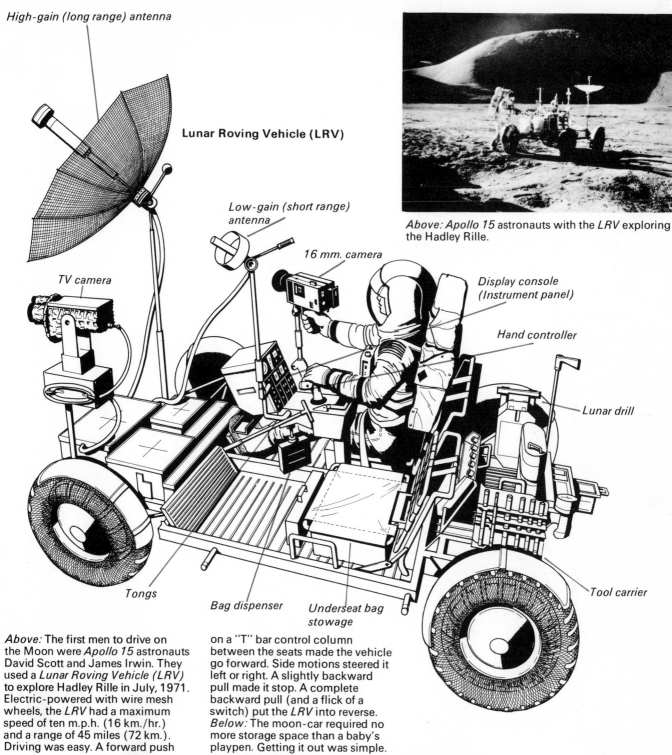

Tongs

Bag dispenser

Underseat bag stowage

Tool carrier

Above: The first men to drive on the Moon were *Apollo 15* astronauts David Scott and James Irwin. They used a *Lunar Roving Vehicle (LRV)* to explore Hadley Rille in July, 1971. Electric-powered with wire mesh wheels, the *LRV* had a maximum speed of ten m.p.h. (16 km./hr.) and a range of 45 miles (72 km.). Driving was easy. A forward push

on a "T" bar control column between the seats made the vehicle go forward. Side motions steered it left or right. A slightly backward pull made it stop. A complete backward pull (and a flick of a switch) put the *LRV* into reverse. *Below:* The moon-car required no more storage space than a baby's playpen. Getting it out was simple.

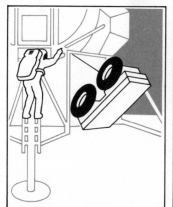

Man in space

Cosmonaut Alexei Leonov painted his pioneer space walk in 1965. He remained attached to the *Voskhod* spacecraft by a safety line, with oxygen bottles strapped to his back

Above: Another scene by Leonov showing the beautiful yet terrifying view from a spacecraft as it re-enters the Earth's atmosphere.

Above: Valentina Tereshkova was a textile worker who took up parachute jumping as a sport and became a cosmonaut. Her epic flight in *Vostok 6* lasted 71 hrs.

Russia's tragic space heroes— Viktor Patsayev, Georgi Dobrovsky and Vladislav Volkov perished when the pressure cabin of their *Soyuz 11* spacecraft became unsealed as they returned to Earth.

Suits to stop blood boiling

No one can live in space—or walk on the Moon or Mars—without the protection of a space suit. Not only does it supply oxygen, but it surrounds the wearer with pressure without which his blood would boil.

The Russian Alexei Leonov was the first to walk in space. After leaving the airlock of his *Voskhod 2* spacecraft on March 18, 1965, he spent ten minutes exercising on the end of a safety line.

Edward H. White II was the first American to walk in space. He remained outside the *Gemini 4* spacecraft for 20 minutes on June 3, 1965. He controlled his actions with the help of a gas-gun.

A spectacular space walk took place in January, 1969, when two Russian *Soyuz* spacecraft docked together in orbit. Two cosmonauts transferred from one ship to the other, and returned to Earth in a different ship.

Protection on the Moon

When Apollo astronauts landed on the Moon they wore more carefully designed space suits. They had to be flexible to allow the wearer to walk, lift, bend, etc. Next to the skin was a liquid-cooling garment with a network of tubes. Water circulated through these tubes to maintain body temperature.

On the Moon the astronaut could sip water through a tube fixed to the neck ring inside the helmet. Toilet facilities for urine collection were provided inside the suit.

The outside of the suit was made of interleaving layers of aluminium and coated nylon and Teflon fabric. These layers were protection against heat and hard wear.

The plastic pressure helmet locked into a ring on the suit. On the top was a coated visor to provide protection from micrometeoroids, thermal radiation and ultraviolet/infrared light. After *Apollo 12*, a sunshade was added to the outer portion of the visor.

Portable Life Support System

The glass fiber backpack supplied oxygen at .26 kgf./per sq. cm. and water to the liquid-cooling garment. The suit atmosphere was kept pure by the use of chemical filters. Radio equipment was also in the backpack.

Special gloves and boots gave protection for clambering over moonrocks and using special tools.

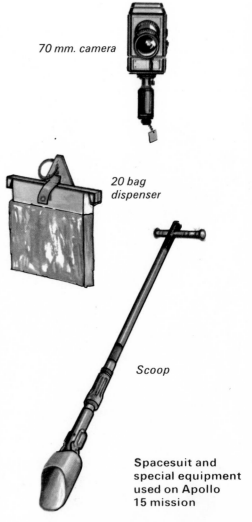

Hammer

PLSS (Back-pack for lunar module pilot)

70 mm. camera

20 bag dispenser

Scoop

Spacesuit and special equipment used on Apollo 15 mission

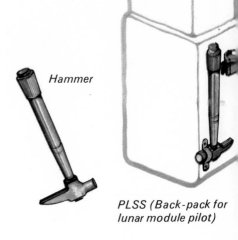

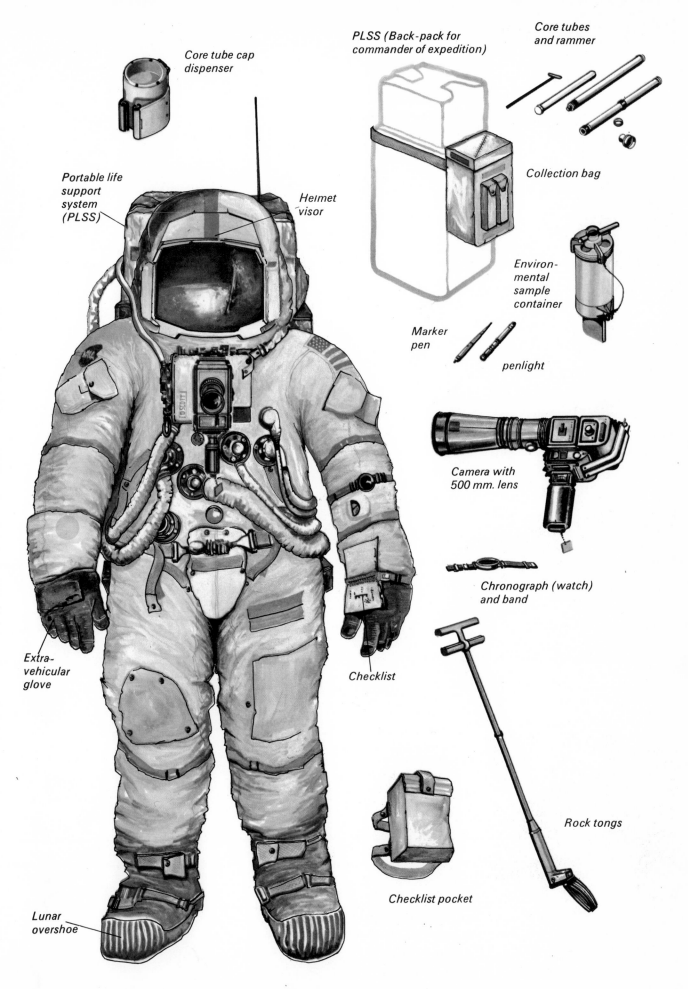

Core tube cap dispenser

PLSS (Back-pack for commander of expedition)

Core tubes and rammer

Portable life support system (PLSS)

Helmet visor

Collection bag

Environmental sample container

Marker pen

penlight

Camera with 500 mm. lens

Chronograph (watch) and band

Extra-vehicular glove

Checklist

Rock tongs

Checklist pocket

Lunar overshoe

Mars the red planet

Above: Statue of Mars from Ancient Rome. Several ancient peoples, including the Romans, linked the planet with blood and war because of its reddish glow. The Romans adopted Mars as one of their Gods. As the Romans became more warlike so did Mars.

A fascinating near neighbor

Mars is only slightly more than half the size of our planet. It has a mythology all its own. The Romans named it after their god of War. When at last astronomers looked at it through telescopes they found that two-thirds of the surface was covered by reddish deserts. They called it "The Red Planet."

In 1877 the Italian astronomer Giovanni Schiaparelli believed he could see faint lines crisscrossing the deserts. This led to the theory—widely believed at the beginning of this century—that intelligent beings on Mars had constructed a vast network of waterways to irrigate their dying planet.

H. G. Wells's famous novel, *War of the Worlds*, published in 1898, described a Martian invasion of Earth. Adapted as a radio play by Orson Welles in 1938, the broadcast caused near-panic in New York. People actually believed creatures from Mars had landed and were advancing on the city with death rays.

Space exploration quickly dispelled these ideas. Close-up television pictures and scientific data from American *Mariner* spacecraft have shown Mars to be a dry, cold, dusty planet with no signs of canals. It has a thin atmosphere consisting mainly of carbon dioxide. Large areas are covered with craters.

Mariner 9 discovered a huge gorge bigger than the Grand Canyon; meandering scars like dry riverbeds, volcanoes, and giant rilles—great splits in the crust which extend for hundreds of miles.

The glistening white polar caps, which shrink in the Martian summer and return in the Martian winter, are mainly carbon-dioxide snow (dry ice) with some water ice mixed in. Water vapor has been found in the atmosphere, particularly over the poles and in low-lying areas.

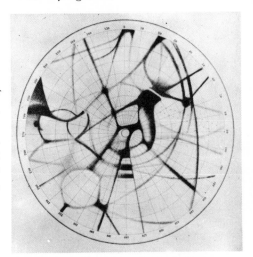

Above: Drawing of Mars by the Italian astronomer Giovanni Schiaparelli.
Below, center and right: Region of Mars taken by *Mariner 9* in January 1972. Right-hand photograph shows a 271 × 346 mile (436 × 557 km.) area with a complex of craters on top of a broad plateau. Center picture shows detail in the small rectangle which suggests flow of lava down slope and away from the central crater group.

Above: Bright objects are seen to fall to Earth at many points. Bizarre creatures emerge from metallic cylinders. The Martians have arrived. Illustration from H. G. Wells' novel *The War of the Worlds.*

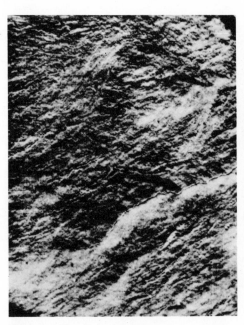

The Viking Project

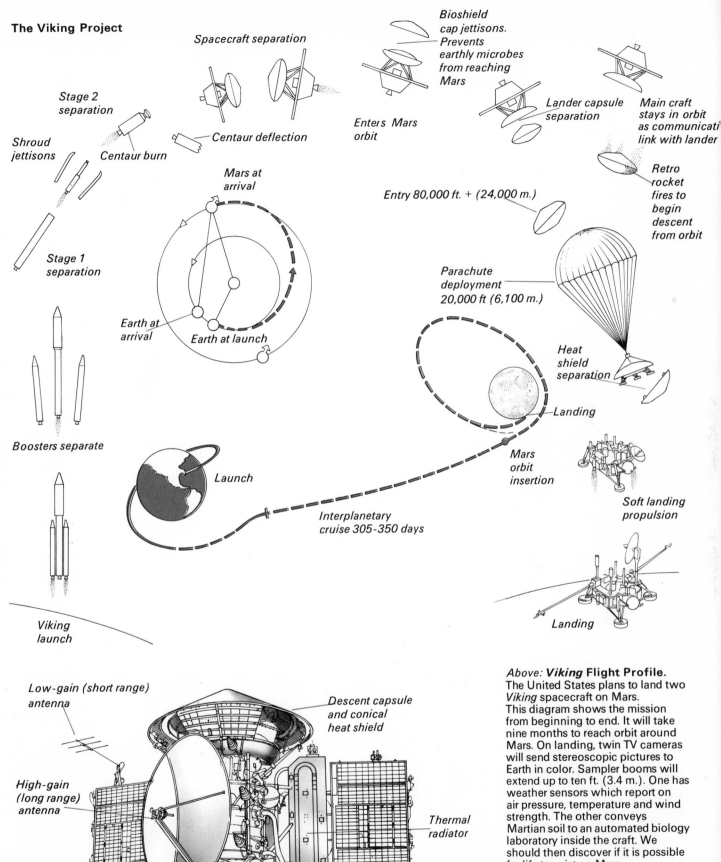

Spacecraft separation

Stage 2 separation

Shroud jettisons

Centaur burn

Centaur deflection

Stage 1 separation

Boosters separate

Viking launch

Bioshield cap jettisons. Prevents earthly microbes from reaching Mars

Enters Mars orbit

Lander capsule separation

Main craft stays in orbit as communicati link with lander

Retro rocket fires to begin descent from orbit

Entry 80,000 ft. + (24,000 m.)

Parachute deployment 20,000 ft (6,100 m.)

Heat shield separation

Landing

Mars at arrival

Earth at arrival

Earth at launch

Launch

Mars orbit insertion

Interplanetary cruise 305-350 days

Soft landing propulsion

Landing

Low-gain (short range) antenna

High-gain (long range) antenna

Descent capsule and conical heat shield

Thermal radiator

Solar cells

Orbital station

Rocket engine

Mars 3

Above: **Viking** Flight Profile. The United States plans to land two *Viking* spacecraft on Mars. This diagram shows the mission from beginning to end. It will take nine months to reach orbit around Mars. On landing, twin TV cameras will send stereoscopic pictures to Earth in color. Sampler booms will extend up to ten ft. (3.4 m.). One has weather sensors which report on air pressure, temperature and wind strength. The other conveys Martian soil to an automated biology laboratory inside the craft. We should then discover if it is possible for life to exist on Mars.

Left: The first soft-landing of an instrument capsule on Mars was achieved by the Soviet *Mars 3* spacecraft on December 2, 1971. It came down in a dust storm and its TV signals lasted only about 20 seconds. The resulting picture was almost blank.

Mercury and Venus the hot planets

Above: Botticelli's famous painting the "Birth of Venus." Venus was the Goddess of Love symbolizing spring and fruitfulness.

Above: Mercury passing in front of the Sun. Both inner planets occasionally do this. Such an event is known as a transit.

The baby of the Sun's family

Mercury is the smallest known planet of the Solar System. It is slightly less than half the Earth's diameter. Mercury is also the closest planet to the Sun and turns on its axis very slowly—once in about 58½ Earth-days. Its rocky surface is alternately baked by the Sun and frozen by the cold of outer space. Because it is a small body with a low gravity it is virtually airless.

Mercury is difficult to see in Earth's sky because it sets so close to sunrise and sunset.

Bright star or UFO.

Venus, on the other hand, is the brightest object in the night sky apart from the Moon. Its sudden appearance behind moving clouds has often led to reports of Unidentified Flying Objects (UFO's). Sometimes it is the evening star crossing the sky as the Sun sets; at other times it is the morning star rising before dawn.

The surface of Venus cannot be seen directly because it is always hidden by thick white clouds. Only when radar signals were reflected from the planet was it possible to find a fixed point of reference. From this the rotation rate could be reliably measured. Venus was found to be turning slowly on its axis in the reverse direction to Earth once every 243 Earth-days. The radar measurements, made by the 210 ft. (64 m.) radio telescope at Goldstone, California, indicated a rough, possibly mountainous surface.

The dense atmosphere of Venus is mainly carbon dioxide which, like a greenhouse, retains much of the Sun's heat.

First direct measurements of the atmosphere of Venus, from the inside, were made by Soviet instrument capsules separated from *Venera* spacecraft. Parachuting deep into the atmosphere, they encountered pressures between 70 and 110 times higher than those on Earth and temperatures high enough to melt lead.

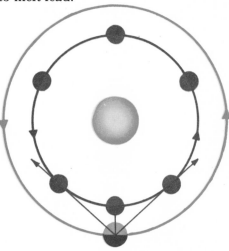

Above: Seen from Earth Venus never appears more than 48° East or West of the Sun.

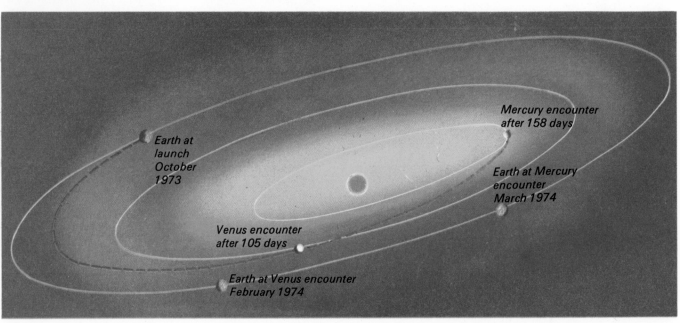

Earth at launch October 1973

Mercury encounter after 158 days

Earth at Mercury encounter March 1974

Venus encounter after 105 days

Earth at Venus encounter February 1974

Venera 4

Above: **First spacecraft to land on Venus.** The 3.28 ft. (1 meter) diameter instrument capsule parachuted into the atmosphere of Venus from Russia's *Venera 4* spacecraft in 1967. On top is the aerial of the radio transmitter which sent data, allowing scientists to find the pressure and temperature.

Right: The journey from Earth to Venus lasted about four months. On the first three attempts signals stopped several miles above the surface (it was thought the very high atmospheric pressure had pushed in the lid of the instrument compartment). At last the capsule of *Venera 7* succeeded in December, 1970. It sent data from the surface for 23 minutes.

Right: Method of soft-landing an instrument capsule from Russia's *Venera* spacecraft. Key: 1. Start of communications session with Earth before penetrating outer atmosphere of Venus; 2. Capsule separates from parent spacecraft (which is destroyed in atmosphere); 3. Capsule slowed by atmospheric drag; 4. Braking parachute opens; 5. Main parachute is pulled out and capsule starts transmitting data to Earth; 6. Radio altimeter measures height from surface; 7. Capsule softlands on Venus.

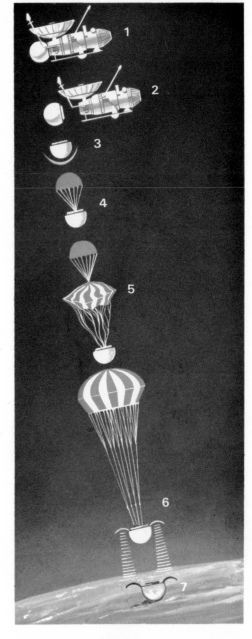

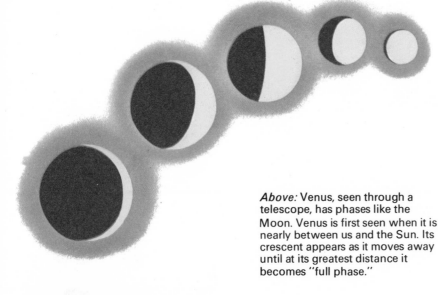

Above: Venus, seen through a telescope, has phases like the Moon. Venus is first seen when it is nearly between us and the Sun. Its crescent appears as it moves away until at its greatest distance it becomes "full phase."

Left: The United States plans to send a *Mariner* spacecraft on a double mission to Venus and Mercury in October/November, 1973. The craft will travel around the Sun until it flies within 3,000 miles (4,800 km.) of Venus in February, 1974. At this distance the planet's gravitation and orbital speed will act like a "sling shot" to propel the craft on to Mercury two months later.

Mariner

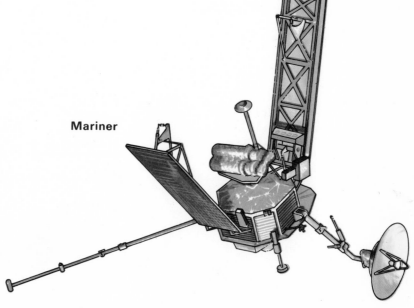

Right: The 900 lb. (408 kg.) *Mariner* craft was designed to send television pictures of both planets as well as data on magnetic fields, space radiation and planetary temperatures, etc.

The outer planets

Above: A statue from Hungary of god Jupiter. He was the most important and powerful god in ancient Rome. Jupiter was lord of the sky and daylight and the sender of thunder and lightning.

Jupiter and beyond

Jupiter is the Goliath of our Solar System. It is more than ten times Earth's diameter, and almost twice the mass of all the rest of the planets put together. Twelve moons are known. The four largest—Io, Europa, Ganymede and Callisto—were discovered by Galileo in 1610 and can easily be seen with a small telescope. Three are bigger than our Moon.

Saturn is the beautiful ringed planet. It, too, is very large and probably much like Jupiter in composition. It has ten moons. One of them, Titan, is about 3,000 miles (4,800 km.) across and has a thin atmosphere.

Uranus spins very fast, once in nearly 11 hours. Strangely, its axis is tilted at more than 90° (the other planets have spin axes almost perpendicular to the planes of their orbits). Physically, it is probably similar to Jupiter and Saturn. There are five moons.

Neptune is almost a twin of Uranus—recent observations suggest it is slightly bigger—but it is nearly half as far from the Sun. The temperature on Neptune must be about −220°C, and almost all its atmosphere must be frozen into ice crystals. It has two moons.

Pluto pursues an eccentric path swinging out to a maximum distance of 4,566 million miles (7,200 million km.) and back within the orbit of Neptune. It may once have been a moon of Neptune.

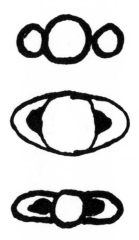

Above: When Galileo first noticed Saturn's rings in 1609-10, they were at a narrow angle and not well displayed. Drawings made at different times reflected his difficulty in understanding the true nature of the planet.

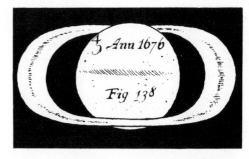

Above: Hevelius thought the planet had two lumpy "star-like" appendages. In 1655, Christian Huygens finally discovered that Saturn possessed a ring system detached from the planet. This drawing was done by another astronomer, Jean Domenique Cassini.

Right: The internal structure of Saturn is probably similar to that of Jupiter. Though far bigger than Earth, it is composed of very light materials, apart from the core which may be of metallic hydrogen under fantastic pressure.

Saturn's rings are 170,000 miles (274,000 km.) wide and about ten miles (16 km.) thick. They probably consist of millions of particles from a moon or moons which came too close to the planet and broke up. Particles may be coated with or made of solid ammonia. The three rings are called the outer ring, the inner ring and (nearest the planet) the crêpe ring. The gap between the two main rings, known as the Cassini division, is 3,000 miles (4,800 km.) across.

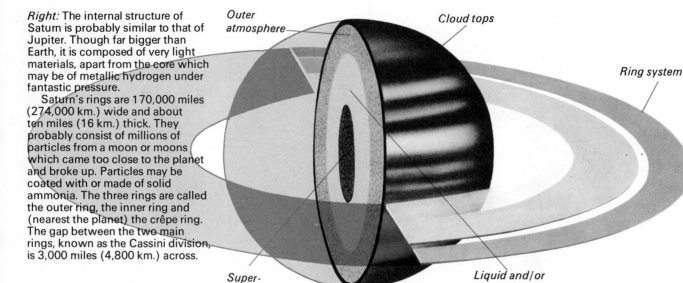

Outer atmosphere — Cloud tops — Ring system — Super-dense core — Liquid and/or solid hydrogen

Saturn

Jupiter

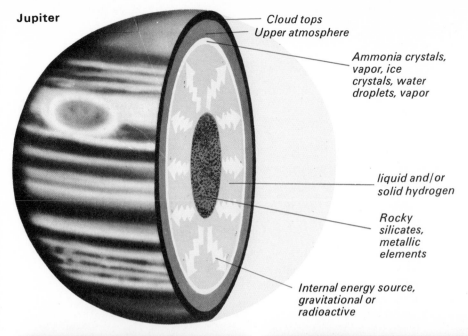

Cloud tops
Upper atmosphere

Ammonia crystals,
vapor, ice
crystals, water
droplets, vapor

liquid and/or
solid hydrogen

Rocky
silicates,
metallic
elements

Internal energy source,
gravitational or
radioactive

Left: Jupiter may be a ball of super-condensed metallic elements encased in a liquid/gaseous envelope. The fast rotation rate of only about ten hours causes bulging at the equator and flattening at the poles, giving the appearance of a slightly oval body. Gases in the clouds form slate blue and salmon pink bands around the planet. The famous "Red Spot," which can easily be seen through a telescope, moves around more slowly and from time to time changes in shape and size. It is sometimes about 30,000 miles (48,000 km.) long and 10,000 miles (16,000 km.) wide—big enough to "swallow" our Earth. The giant planet periodically sends out huge bursts of radio noise which can be picked up by radio telescopes. It may also be the only planet in the Solar System which radiates more energy than it absorbs from the Sun.

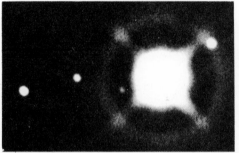

(1) **URANUS,** the first planet to be discovered by telescope, was found by William Herschel in 1781 while he was making a systematic examination of the stars.

(2) **NEPTUNE,** last of the giant planets, was discovered in 1846 by J. Galle and H. d'Arrest, Berlin Observatory after two other astronomers, Urbain Leverrier in France and John C. Adams in England, had predicted mathematically where it could be found.

(3) **PLUTO** was discovered in 1930 by Clyde Tombaugh after Percival Lowell and others had predicted the ninth planet because of the changes in the orbits of Uranus and Neptune.

Above: Urbain Jean Joseph Leverrier (1811-1877) of France was the professional planet-hunter. He studied comets and the way in which their paths were changed (perturbed) by the gravitational pull of the Sun and other bodies. His precise orbit calculations led to the discovery of Neptune.

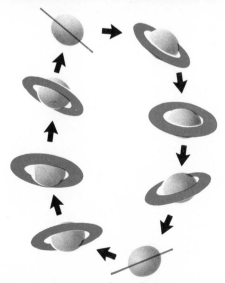

Changing aspects of Saturn's rings, as seen from Earth. Sometimes the rings are edgewise-on and almost invisible.

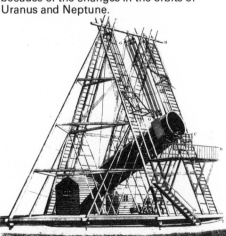

Above: Reflecting telescope built by William Herschel.

Above: Sir William Herschel (1738-1822) began his professional life as a musician. He became private astronomer to Great Britain's King George III and is remembered as the best telescope-maker of the 18th century.

Interplanetary travel in the future

Right: Pioneer 10 was the first spacecraft destined to travel beyond the Solar System toward the stars. It left Cape Kennedy on March 2, 1972. After a flight of — nearly two years it is expected to pass within 90,000 miles of Jupiter to send pictures and scientific data back to Earth. A whiplash effect, produced by the giant planet's gravity and orbital speed, will then accelerate the craft on its way toward the edge of the Solar System and beyond.

On board is a special message designed to last at least 100 million years, in case *Pioneer 10* is ever found by an alien civilization. Drawings of a man and a woman to scale with a Pioneer spacecraft were etched on a 6×9 in. (152×229 m.) sheet of gold anodized aluminium. The man's hand is outstretched in a gesture of greeting. Other drawings indicate Earth's position in the Solar System, and the Solar System's position in the Galaxy. The approximate time when the launch was made is given by the positions of known pulsars—the remnants of supernovae (exploding stars). *Below:* (1) The route of *Pioneer 10*.

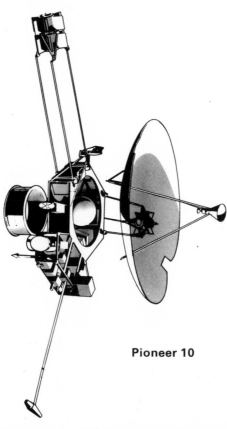

Pioneer 10

In the late 1970's a rare alignment of all five of the outer planets of our Solar System will allow spacecraft to be sent on Grand Tours.
Below: The United States had planned to send spacecraft on two different flight paths, as shown in the diagram (below), using the gravitational pull and orbital velocity of one planet to whip them on to the next. This "sling-shot" technique cuts the journey time to the outer planets—normally about 18 years—in half. One mission (2) was to have passed Jupiter, Uranus and Neptune; the other (3) Jupiter, Saturn and Pluto. Along the way on-board TV cameras and scientific instruments were to have observed the planets and the various moons, reporting back by radio.

Although the project was abandoned as "too expensive for the expected scientific gain," the Soviets may yet make the attempt. The opportunity will not occur again for another 170 years because of the slow movement of the outer planets around the Sun.

The only alternative is to give spacecraft more efficient engines which speed up the journey. In January, 1972, it was announced that the United States was studying a small 15,000 lb. (6,804 kg.) thrust atomic engine that might be used on unmanned missions to the outer planets in the 1980's.

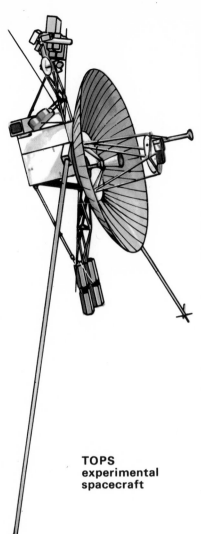

TOPS experimental spacecraft

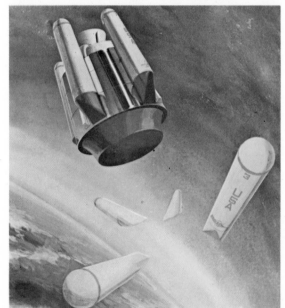

Above: Manned expeditions to Mars cannot be expected before the end of the century. This is an artist's impression of the Deimos project studied by McDonnell Douglas in the United States. Mars explorers leave their mother ship in orbit and descend to the surface in landing crafts similar to the Apollo lunar module, taking with them roving vehicles and a full range of exploration gear. When they have finished their work they will launch themselves back to the mother ship for the journey home.

Left: Expeditions such as the Deimos project would require huge spaceships assembled in Earth-orbit to carry explorers and expedition vehicles on round trips lasting 18 months or more. The spaceship is discarding fuel tanks at escape velocity as it departs from Earth.

Above: The TOPS experimental spacecraft which only reached model stage. This was the design for the craft planned to make the Grand Tour in the late 1970's.

Right: **Spaceship Discovery.** One of the many space vehicle designs specially created by space engineers Frederick Ordway and Harry Lange for the M-G-M Cinerama epic film, *2001: A Space Odyssey.* The craft was 700 ft. (213 m.) long. It was intended to carry explorers into orbit around Jupiter. Atomic engines were at the rear, and a spherical nose-section housed the crew. Inside the pressurized nose was a centrifuge in which the crew enjoyed Earth-like gravity conditions created by spin. Controlling the mission was the incredible HAL 9000 "talking computer." Beneath the flight deck was the pod bay with three one-man spacecraft with arm-like manipulators. The pods were used for outside inspection, maintenance and repair of the mother ship. In the film one was also used in an attempt to rescue an astronaut stranded in space.

Asteroids, comets and meteors

Ceres compares in size with Italy. It is the largest of the asteroids, or "minor planets," and orbits the Sun beyond Mars. It was discovered in 1801.

Below: Halley's Comet as it appears in the famous Bayeux tapestry. Throughout history men have believed the appearance of comets to mean that some terrible disaster was about to occur. No doubt a comet's appearance disturbing the natural order of the heavens was linked with similar happenings on earth. In 1066, just before the Norman invasion, Halley's comet was sighted. People associated it with King Harold's defeat and death at the Battle of Hastings.

The asteroids or minor planets

There are many more objects in the Solar System than planets and moons. For example, between the orbits of Mars and Jupiter are the asteroids or minor planets. They may be the remains of a planet which failed to form or, after forming, broke up. These bodies range from small particles to immense irregular rocks. The largest, Ceres, is 480 miles (772 km.) across.

Not all the minor planets move in a tight band. Some emerge on highly deviating paths both toward and away from the Sun. In 1937 Hermes, less than a mile (1.6 km.) across, came within 500,000 miles (805,000 km.) of the Earth; Eros is expected to pass within 15 million miles (24.1 million km.) in 1975. Icarus actually dips inside the orbit of Mercury close to the Sun before departing for a point beyond the orbit of Mars.

Spacecraft sent to explore Jupiter and the outer planets have to cruise through the asteroid belt. They are unlikely to collide with rocks the size of footballs or even green peas. The danger comes from the far greater number of particles from 1/10th to 1/1000th of a gram. Near the Earth, meteoroids with a mass of 1/100th gram traveling at 33,600 m.p.h. (54,000 km./hr.) relative to the spacecraft, can penetrate a single sheet of aluminium one centimeter thick. At Jupiter such particles travel at only about 15,600 m.p.h. (25,200 km./hr.).

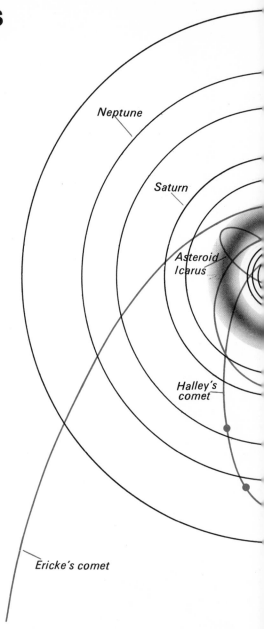

Neptune

Saturn

Asteroid Icarus

Halley's comet

Ericke's comet

Comets

Comets are the real wanderers of the Solar System. Only occasionally is one seen, but a good sighting can be spectacular. It appears as a bright ball of light with a long, glowing tail. Night after night it can be seen moving against the background of stars until it fades away. Some comets enter the Solar System, travel around the Sun and depart again, never to return. Others are regular visitors through the centuries.

The head of a comet is probably composed of rock particles, dust and ice. As it approaches the Sun, the ices evaporate without melting. The resulting tail always points away from the Sun because of solar radiation pressure and the effect of the solar wind.

Each time a comet passes the Sun it loses some of its substance. In the end only dust particles remain.

The Meteor Crater in Arizona is nearly a mile wide (1,600 m.) and 600 ft. (182 m.) deep in solid rock. The body causing this crater must have weighed over a million tons. The crater is probably at least 10,000 years old.

Path of a meteor across the sky. It is seen exploding as it descends through the atmosphere.

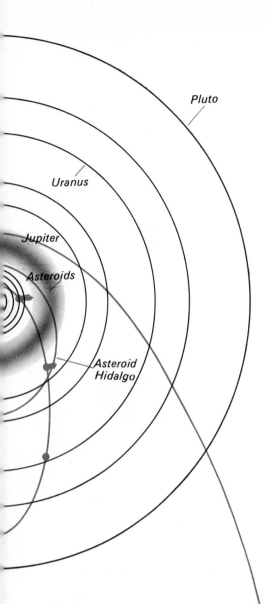

Above: Simplified diagram of the solar system showing paths of certain asteroids and comets.

Meteors and Meteorites

Almost everyone must have seen a meteor or shooting star—a spear of light that suddenly appears and dies away. It is, of course, not a star at all. It is a piece of stone or iron which has entered the Earth's atmosphere at immense speed (perhaps 45 miles [72 km.] per second) and has been burned up by friction with the air.

Most meteors are caused by tiny particles no bigger than a grain of sand. Larger pieces which reach the ground are called meteorites. On its journey around the Sun, the Earth captures millions of them every year. The most likely explanation is that they are debris left over from the formation of the Solar System and dust particles from comets.

The really big ones that reach the Earth range in size from small pebbles to huge blocks, weighing many tons. One that fell in Arizona in prehistoric times left a crater nearly a mile (1.6 km.) wide and 600 ft. (182 m.) deep.

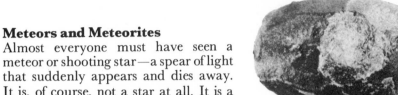

Above: An example of a meteorite.

Below: The remains of comets produce spectacular meteor displays when they intersect Earth's orbit. A good example are the Leonids which pursue an elliptical path around the Sun. Particles from the swarm were estimated to have pelted the Earth with a quarter of a million meteors in nine hours in 1833. Spectacular displays were also observed in 1866 and 1966.

Above: Photograph of comet. The tail may be up to about 200 million miles (320 million km.) long.

Below: Paths that comets follow around the Sun. Comets traveling hyperbolic and parabolic paths are lost from the Solar System.

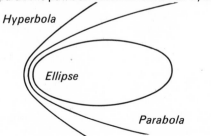

Observing the stars

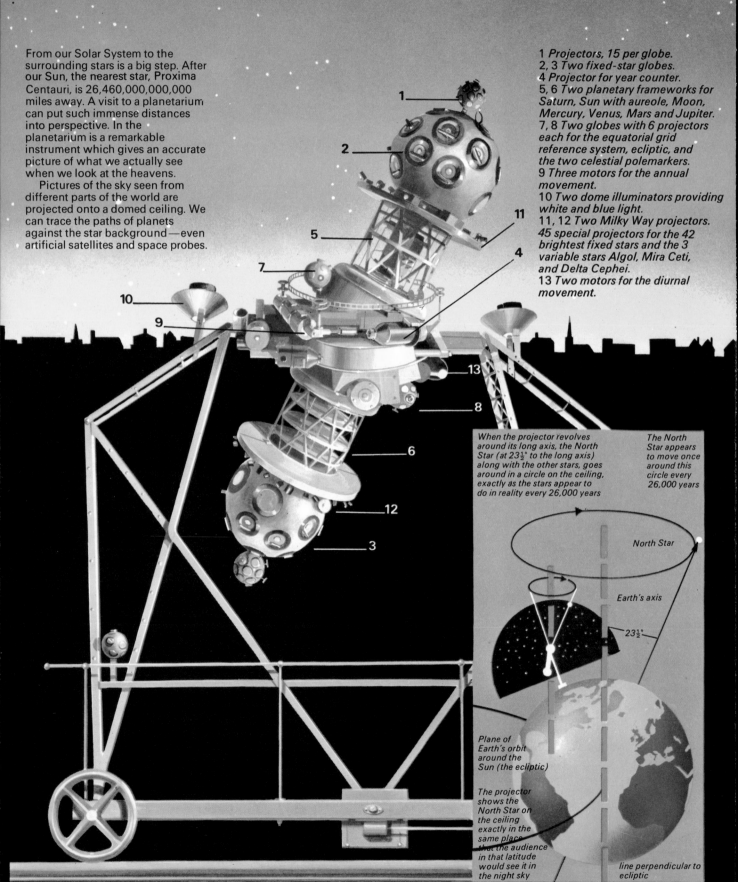

From our Solar System to the surrounding stars is a big step. After our Sun, the nearest star, Proxima Centauri, is 26,460,000,000,000 miles away. A visit to a planetarium can put such immense distances into perspective. In the planetarium is a remarkable instrument which gives an accurate picture of what we actually see when we look at the heavens.

Pictures of the sky seen from different parts of the world are projected onto a domed ceiling. We can trace the paths of planets against the star background—even artificial satellites and space probes.

1 *Projectors, 15 per globe.*
2, 3 *Two fixed-star globes.*
4 *Projector for year counter.*
5, 6 *Two planetary frameworks for Saturn, Sun with aureole, Moon, Mercury, Venus, Mars and Jupiter.*
7, 8 *Two globes with 6 projectors each for the equatorial grid reference system, ecliptic, and the two celestial polemarkers.*
9 *Three motors for the annual movement.*
10 *Two dome illuminators providing white and blue light.*
11, 12 *Two Milky Way projectors.*
45 special projectors for the 42 brightest fixed stars and the 3 variable stars Algol, Mira Ceti, and Delta Cephei.
13 *Two motors for the diurnal movement.*

When the projector revolves around its long axis, the North Star (at 23½° to the long axis) along with the other stars, goes around in a circle on the ceiling, exactly as the stars appear to do in reality every 26,000 years

The North Star appears to move once around this circle every 26,000 years

North Star

Earth's axis

23½°

Plane of Earth's orbit around the Sun (the ecliptic)

The projector shows the North Star on the ceiling exactly in the same place that the audience in that latitude would see it in the night sky

line perpendicular to ecliptic

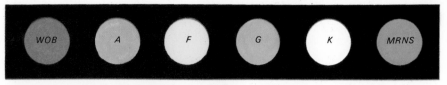

Patterns in the sky

When we look at the night sky through binoculars or a telescope, we can easily tell the difference between stars and planets. The planets present a definite globe-like disc. Stars appear as twinkling points of light.

Early man found he could pick out shapes and patterns in the heavens which looked like the things around him. For example, one group of stars reminded him of a hunter, another a lion.

It was the Romans who gave these star patterns—we call them constellations—their now familiar Latin names. Probably the best known is Ursa Major, the Great Bear, whose main stars form the Plow.

The stars are really suns, as we would soon discover if we could travel beyond our Solar System. Looking back, we would see our sun shrink to a tiny point of light, like the other stars. We know that some nearby stars have planet-like bodies circling them.

Stars, hot and cool

Not all stars are like our Sun. Many are bigger and brighter. Some are very compact and cooler. Astronomers put them into groups, according to their temperature and color. Our sun is a yellow star of Group G.

Some stars, like our own, exist in isolation. Others are tied together by gravitation into groups of two, three and more, revolving around a common center. There are also much larger clusters.

Stars which explode, scattering their contents deep into surrounding space, are called supernovae. Radio astronomers have found that they leave behind collapsed bodies—pulsars—that emit radio waves, light and X-rays that vary in strength several times a second, like a far-off beacon.

If we traveled far enough, we would also discover that our Sun is part of an immense "island" of stars, gas and dust turning slowly in space. We call this the Galaxy.

Looking toward the center, we see the Milky Way where stars are so thickly packed that they appear as one immense band of light. We see only a few of the foreground stars from our tiny planet.

Above: Not all stars are the same. Astronomers have divided them into different groups. Our Sun is a yellow star of Group G. Very hot blue-white stars are W, O and B. Group A (white) and F (yellow-white) are medium-hot. Groups K (orange) and M (orange-red) are medium cool and S are redder and cooler.

Left: **Stars in the making.** Within these dark clouds of gas and dust of the Trifid Nebula in Sagittarius new stars are being born. Radiation from hot early-type stars excite the gas atoms in this colorful nebula which is 30 light years across.

Below: **Birth and death of a Sun-like star.** The star is born when a cloud of interstellar material shrinks, becoming highly compressed and thermonuclear reactions are started, turning hydrogen to helium (1). It starts to shine after 100 million years, shines steadily for 10,000 million years (2) and then, as hydrogen is used up (3), swells to a giant 1,500 times brighter and 50 times larger. Then it becomes unstable (4) and may explode to end its life (5) as a white dwarf.

Right: A map of the constellations drawn by Joannes Janssonius in 1660.

Our Galaxy the milky way

Our Galaxy shown side-on.

Above: Our Galaxy shown side-on. *Right:* The plane view. The arrows show the position of the Solar System.

As our planet is located within the outer disc of the Galaxy—about 30,000 light years from the center—we get a nearly edge-on view of its central regions. At night we see a luminous band which seems to flow across the sky—the Milky Way. Democritus, who lived in Greece in the 5th century BC, supposed it was made up of an enormous number of stars too faint for the eye to see. A small telescope will show that he guessed correctly. The milky appearance of the sky is, in fact, due to the light of multitudes of stars appearing brightest toward the center of the Galaxy.

Right: Martin and Tatiana Teskula at Lund University in Sweden drew this remarkable map of the Milky Way with reference to hundreds of astronomical photographs. Various foreground objects are positioned according to latitude and longitude measurements. The brightest stars seen from Earth lie within a radius of some 3,000 light years. Fainter stars and nebulae are more remote. The Galaxy's central "hub," which lies in the direction of the Constellation Sagittarius, cannot be clearly seen because of obscuring matter—stars, gas and dust—in the spiral arms lying between us and the center. Radio telescopes help to map these regions. Looking out from Earth in the opposite direction, the stars thin out to the edge of the Galaxy. Not shown on this map is the Galaxy's spherical halo which contains globular clusters and older individual stars above and below the disc.

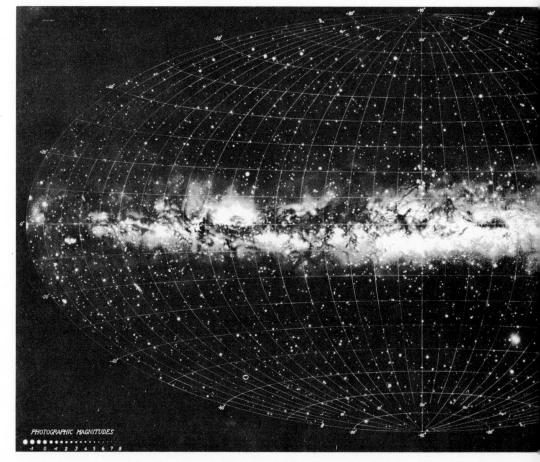

PHOTOGRAPHIC MAGNITUDES

Top right: In the Northern Hemisphere the whole of the sky seems to revolve around Polaris (the Pole Star). Easy to find are the constellations Ursa Major (the Great Bear) and Cassiopeia, shaped like a "W."

With binoculars try to locate the Great Nebula in Andromeda—a "nearby" galaxy far beyond our own "star island." Andromeda extends from one corner of the square of Pegasus which can be found by extending a line from Polaris through Cassiopeia. The galaxy is seen as a hazy spot of light.

Below right: From the Southern Hemisphere we can see other parts of the heavens. Prominent is Crux (the Southern Cross). Orion—which can also be seen in the Northern sky during the summer—has the huge, red star Betelgeuse in one corner. Sirius in Canis Major is impossible to miss. It is the brightest star in the night sky. The constellation Centaurus contains Proxima Centauri, the nearest star beyond the Sun It is just $4\frac{1}{4}$ light years away.

Below: This is a specially constructed photograph showing the complete Milky Way.

The Northern Night Sky

The Southern Night Sky

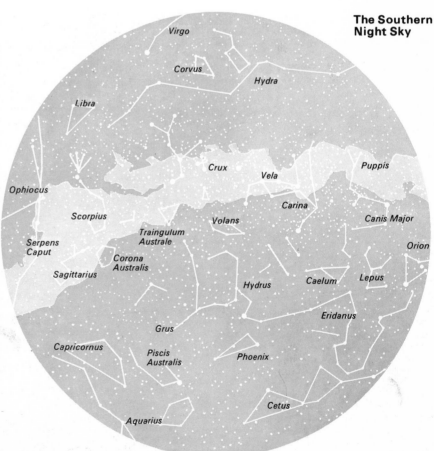

33

The radio sky astronomy by sound

Signals from deep space

The radio telescope owes its origin to Karl G. Jansky. In 1931 he discovered that radio waves were reaching the Earth from outer space. Nobody knew what they were or where they came from.

Grote Reber of Illinois made the first serious attempts to confirm Jansky's findings. He set up the first radio telescope in his garden. Reber's instrument was thirty feet in diameter and designed to receive on a wavelength of about two meters. It could be aimed at any part of the heavens. The instrument showed that signals are strongest near the center of our Galaxy and along the plane of the Milky Way where the stars are most thickly clustered.

Strangely, when the instrument was aimed at individual bright stars, no signals were heard. At first it seemed that a new type of "radio star" had been discovered. Then, during World War II, a young Dutch research student, Van de Hulst, suggested an answer. Perhaps the radio signals originated in the highly rarefied hydrogen clouds of interstellar space.

This was confirmed in 1948 when John G. Bolton and Gordon J. Stanley in Sydney, Australia, and Ryle and Smith in Cambridge, England, announced at almost the same time that radio waves were coming from localized sources in space. One was in the constellation of Cygnus, another in Cassiopeia. Then, in 1951, radio astronomers in the United States, Australia and Holland detected weak signals from the hydrogen cloud in the Milky Way.

More discoveries followed. It was found that radio waves were coming from the gaseous remnants of supernovae, "exploding stars" like the Crab Nebula and from a position where Tycho Brahe had seen a supernova in 1572. Radio telescopes began to open up entirely new fields of astronomy.

How the Radio Telescope works

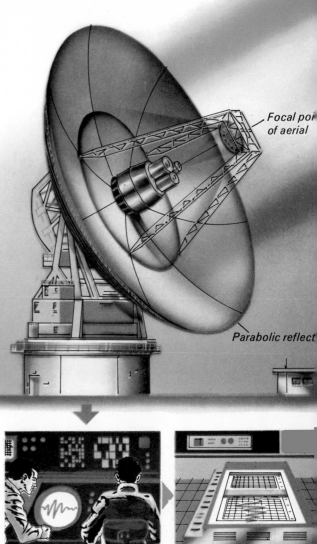

Focal point of aerial

Parabolic reflector

Steerable radio telescopes have large dishes or paraboloids. They are designed to move on a circular horizontal path and also to tilt. By a combination of these movements they can point anywhere in the sky. Typical subjects for study are the interstellar gas clouds, nebulae, pulsars, radio galaxies and quasars. Incoming signals are collected by the dish and reflected to the aerial or feed situated at the focal point. Intensity varies as the telescope scans across the radio source. Signals are fed to a detector amplifier (1) and recorded within the observatory by means of a pen recorder (2) which produces a trace on a graph. Signals are also recorded on tape (3) and may be fed to a computer (4) for analysis.

Right: The Mk 1 radio-telescope at Jodrell Bank, Cheshire, has a 250 ft (76 m) dish. The giant instrument can be pointed at any part of the sky to pick up natural radio waves from stars, nebulae, supernovae, pulsars, quasars, etc. Completed in 1957, it also enabled Britain to track and communicate with artificial satellites and space probes.

Radio waves from source of radio energy e.g. hydrogen clouds, pulsar, radio galaxy, quasar, etc.

Right: This "merry-go-round" aerial contraption led to one of the greatest discoveries of modern astronomy. Set up by Karl Jansky on a farm in New Jersey in 1931, it was meant to investigate the causes of static—the hiss and crackle that came from early radio sets. Its wheels came from an old Ford automobile, and it was made to revolve by a motor. While operating the aerial, Jansky became aware of certain radio emissions which seemed to come from the sky. By accident, Jansky had built the first crude radio telescope.

Right: Radio telescopes can also be used as radar transmitters. For example, when a meteor enters the atmosphere it leaves a trail of ionized gases which reflect radio waves. The object can be easily located from the signals reflected back.

Above: The Arecibo radio telescope in Puerto Rico is four times the diameter of the Jodrell Bank dish, but is non-steerable. It was designed and built by Cornell University at a cost of $8 million in a natural bowl formed by several mountain peaks. After the ground was sculptured into the shape of a paraboloid, a wire-mesh reflector made of separate panels was set in place. There is a focusing device 500 ft. (152 m.) above the reflector which can be moved along cables.

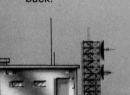

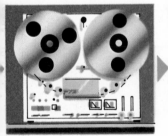

Right: To achieve a world-wide space tracking system, the Soviet Union has special ships which can be stationed in the Atlantic, Pacific and Indian Oceans. The flagship, *Kosmonaut Yuri Gagarin,* is the world's largest research ship. It is 758 ft. (232 m.) long, 102 ft. (31 m.) wide, has a displacement of 45,000 tons and a speed of 18 knots. The ship has an automatic telephone exchange, a 300-seat amphitheater for films and lectures, rest rooms, three swimming pools (one heated), and a large gym.

Galaxies in the making

For a long time astronomers thought the Milky Way was the whole of Creation. Only when powerful telescopes came into use early in this century did we begin to see how big the Universe is.

Misty patches in the night sky thought to lie within our own Galaxy had been called nebulae. The big telescopes began to show that some of them were, in fact, other galaxies far beyond our own. Nowadays the term nebula is only used for the clouds of gas and dust that really are part of our system, like the Trifid Nebula in Sagittarius and the Great Nebula in Orion.

It is still not clear how galaxies form. They seem to begin life as huge irregular clouds of hydrogen which grow together and gradually become localized centers of turbulent gas. As more and more gas is pulled in by gravitation, instability within the cloud causes it to rotate.

Not all galaxies assume the familiar spiral form. Some are spirals with central bars. Others are irregular, lens-shaped or globular. The differences depend on how far they have evolved, how fast they rotate, and the size of magnetic forces. Sometimes the appearance is deceptive because of the angle at which they present themselves to the telescope. Seen edge-on, a spiral galaxy looks like a line of light with a central bulge.

The galaxies tend to be irregularly scattered throughout space, though some are bound together in immense clusters. Our own system is part of a cluster of 27 which includes the Andromeda spiral two million light years away.

More than 6,000 million galaxies can be observed with the 200-inch telescope, and our own galaxy contains well over 100,000 million stars!

To the end of the Universe

We know that the Universe is expanding. Light waves coming from a distant galaxy are lengthened as a result of the galaxy's relative motion away from us; its whole spectrum is moved slightly towards the red. By measuring this movement we can find the speed at which the galaxy is moving away. This is the law of the Red Shift.

In remote space radio astronomers have found bodies which they call *quasars* (quasi-stellar or apparently star-like objects). If the Red Shift theory holds for such bodies, they must be near the limit of the observable Universe. They produce radio waves and light of tremendous power yet seem to be incredibly compact bodies. One theory is that they are spinning magnetic relics of galaxies. Galaxies near the limits of the 200-inch telescope—at a distance of 5,000 million light years—are receding at nearly half the speed of light. Those at more than twice this distance will be moving away from us with a speed greater than light. Their emissions cannot break through to us against the expansion that is taking place. If the Red Shift law can be applied at such great distances, this is the boundary of the Universe we can observe.

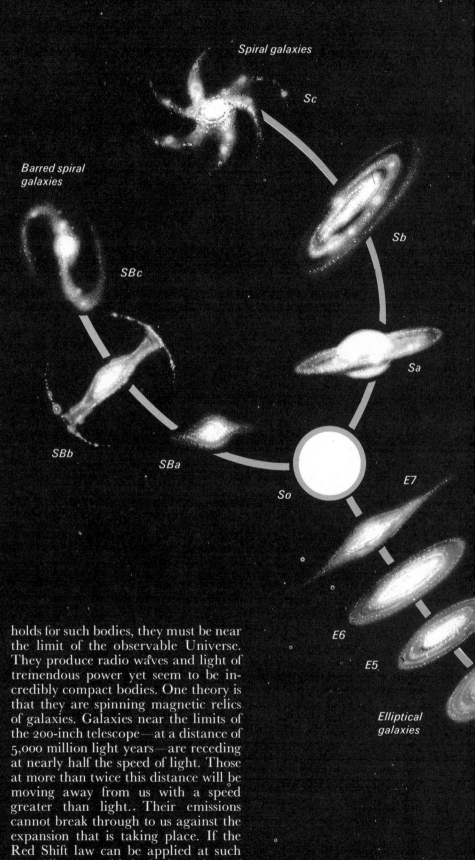

Spiral galaxies

Sc

Sb

Sa

Barred spiral galaxies

SBc

SBb

SBa

So

E7

E6

E5

Elliptical galaxies

Types of Galaxies

The great American astronomer Edwin Hubble (1889-1953) classified the galaxies into three main types: barred spiral, spiral and elliptical. A few others which have no special shape were called irregular.

Some of the brightest galaxies are elliptical, but spiral forms usually have much greater diameters. Many of the stars in the discs of spirals are bluer, hotter and younger than those in elliptical galaxies. The latter are generally redder and older with less hydrogen gas and dust between the stars.

At first it was supposed that galaxies began life as spirals and gradually condensed into elliptical form. Today we appreciate that the story is not quite so simple.

We must also take into account the effects of powerful forces set up within galaxies which help to shape them.

Barred spirals are divided into Types SBa, SBb and SBc. The difference depends on the balance between magnetic forces within the galaxy and the speed with which it rotates.

Spiral galaxies are formed without central bars when magnetic fields are small compared with rotational forces. Types Sa and Sb have larger nuclei and less pronounced spiral form; type Sc has a smaller nucleus and the spiral effect is more pronounced.

Elliptical galaxies range from the almost spherical E0 type to the elliptical E7 type. The more elliptical forms have faster rotation. Linking the different galactic types was assumed to be the type So galaxy. This was more of a flattened ellipse than the E7 but without spiral form.

E4

E3

E2

Rounder galaxies, redder and cooler

E1

E0

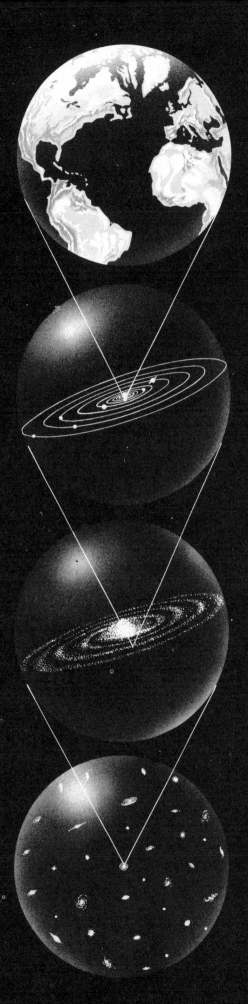

The Earth and the Moon are nearly a quarter of a million miles apart. Light (or radio waves) takes 1.3 seconds to cover this distance.

The Solar System is about 8,000 million miles (13,000 million km.) across the disc. Light takes about 8.3 minutes to travel from the Sun to the Earth; and about 5.5 hours to reach Pluto.

The Galaxy is 100,000 light years across (one light year is the distance traveled by light in one year) and 20,000 light years deep at the center.

The Universe we can observe is limited to a distance of about 10,000 million light years. We cannot detect galaxies which are receding from us faster than the velocity of light.

How the universe began early ideas

Throughout recorded history people have wondered how the Universe was created. The starry heavens were a constant source of fascination. So were terrifying acts of Nature, like thunder and lightning. What people could not explain they attributed to the gods or other supernatural forces. Many ancient myths have come down to us through the ages.

Above: The Egyptian sky goddess Nut whose supple body supports the arched roof of the heavens. Across her body travel the Sun and the Moon producing the pattern of night and day. She is supported by Shu, the god of air. At his feet is Geb, earth-god and husband of Nut.

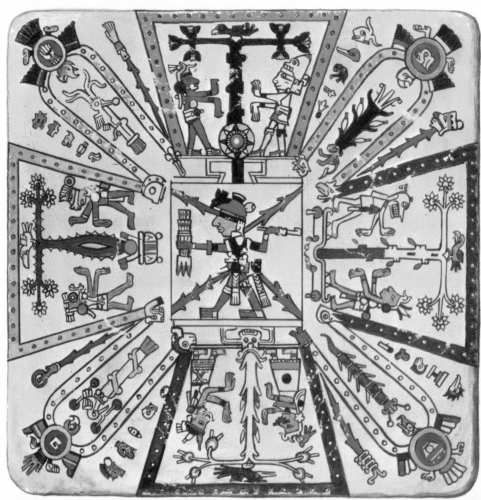

Left: Indian totem pole from the northwest coast of North America. The Thunderbird at the top is the huge supernatural creature whose wings, according to Indian belief, produce the rolling thunder and whose eyes produce lightning.

Above: The five world regions according to Aztec mythology. They are associated with the four sons of Ometecuhtli who created the world. At the center is the present world, representing instability, in which earthquakes are created.

Above: Cosmic mirror from the T'ang dynasty (618–907 A.D.) of ancient China in which the Creation is symbolized by mountains north, south, east and west formed by the body of P'an-ku, the "first man on Earth."

Above: The god Maui pulling up land from the ocean for people to live on. In Polynesian mythology, he is also credited with championing people against the gods and with stealing fire for them from the keeper of the underworld.

Above: The god Thor, creator of the world in Teutonic mythology. He was also the Thunder god. This drawing was made from a bronze statuette found in Northern Iceland. Thor is seated on a throne with the hammer Mjolnir across his knees.

Right: God created the world in six days; on the seventh day God rested, according to the Book of Genesis. The seven days are illustrated in this section of an initial letter in a 13th century illuminated manuscript, beginning at the top with the separation of light from darkness.

The nature of the universe modern ideas

What we know about the Universe
The Universe includes all created matter—the Earth, our Sun, the Solar System, the distant stars and all the galaxies. No one knows how big the Universe is, whether it has any limits, or how it began. We know it is expanding. All galaxies (actually groups of galaxies) are moving steadily apart. The farthest galaxies we can see are moving away at more than half the speed of light. This expansion has led astronomers to believe that the Universe must have begun at a single point. In our diagrams each dot represents a group of galaxies.

The Big Bang Theory (top sequence) holds that a primeval atom. or "cosmic egg," exploded, creating in a single act all the matter in the Universe. The high temperatures produced the elements which formed into galaxies forever moving apart. The Theory depends on evidence that galaxies at great distances appear to be more numerous than galaxies near us. Calculations suggest the "great cosmic explosion" happened ten to 20 thousand million years ago.

The Pulsating Universe Theory (center sequence). This assumes that the Universe is alternately expanding and contracting. If this is true, the Universe we observe is in a period of expansion. When the limit is reached, the whole of created matter will again contract until the galaxies are squeezed so tightly together that another cosmic explosion renews the expansion cycle.

The Steady State Theory (bottom sequence) is quite different. It holds that hydrogen atoms, which eventually form into new galaxies, are being continually created throughout the Universe. As older galaxies move apart, new galaxies form to fill the spaces so that, in any period of time, the Universe looks very much the same. According to the original estimate by British astronomer Fred Hoyle (who proposed the Theory in conjunction with Herman Bondi and Thomas Gold), one atom of hydrogen per year in a volume equal to St. Paul's Cathedral would be enough to account for the Universe we know. This Universe would have no beginning and no end.

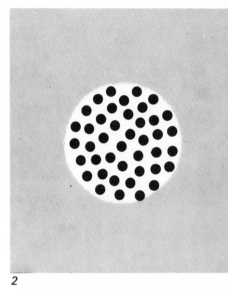
1

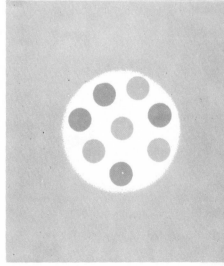
2

1

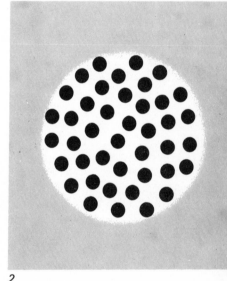
2

1

2

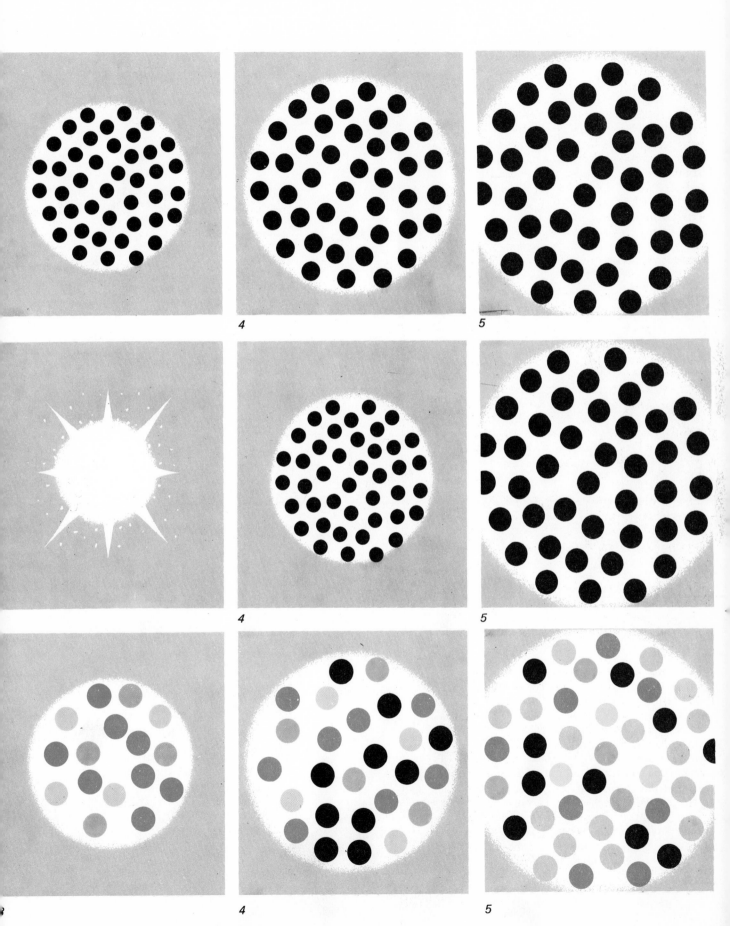

4

5

4

5

3

4

5

Space travel the next steps

The space shuttle approved by President Nixon on January 5, 1972, consists of two major units, the boosters and the orbiter. The orbiter will be launched into space through the simultaneous burning of its solid-propellant boosters and its own main engines. The boosters will detach at an altitude of about 25 miles (40 km.) leaving the orbiter, with its crew of four and cargo, to continue into orbit under its own power.

Below: An alternative design had a simplified liquid-propellant pressure-fed rocket which came down in the Atlantic by parachutes.

Right: The approved solid type will also be recovered by parachute. In each case the winged orbiter will be attached to a big tank from whicn it will draw liquid-oxygen and liquid-hydrogen propellants. The tank will be discarded in orbit.

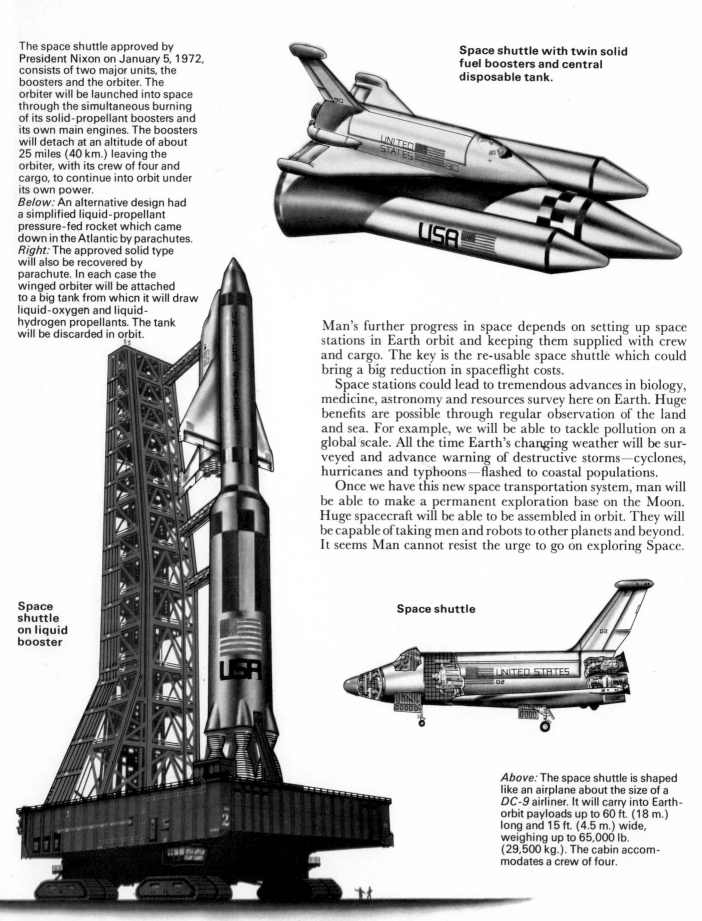

Space shuttle with twin solid fuel boosters and central disposable tank.

Space shuttle on liquid booster

Space shuttle

Man's further progress in space depends on setting up space stations in Earth orbit and keeping them supplied with crew and cargo. The key is the re-usable space shuttle which could bring a big reduction in spaceflight costs.

Space stations could lead to tremendous advances in biology, medicine, astronomy and resources survey here on Earth. Huge benefits are possible through regular observation of the land and sea. For example, we will be able to tackle pollution on a global scale. All the time Earth's changing weather will be surveyed and advance warning of destructive storms—cyclones, hurricanes and typhoons—flashed to coastal populations.

Once we have this new space transportation system, man will be able to make a permanent exploration base on the Moon. Huge spacecraft will be able to be assembled in orbit. They will be capable of taking men and robots to other planets and beyond. It seems Man cannot resist the urge to go on exploring Space.

Above: The space shuttle is shaped like an airplane about the size of a *DC-9* airliner. It will carry into Earth-orbit payloads up to 60 ft. (18 m.) long and 15 ft. (4.5 m.) wide, weighing up to 65,000 lb. (29,500 kg.). The cabin accommodates a crew of four.

Above: If a manned, fully re-usable aircraft-type booster could be used to launch the space shuttle, operating costs could be reduced still further. This drawing shows a Lockheed design for a manned flyback booster releasing the shuttle orbiter high in the stratosphere. The booster uses hydrogen-fueled air-breathing engines, rather than rocket engines.

Above: This is a design for a manned space station proposed for the 1980's. The central area contains crew accommodation, including a galley, centrifuge and gymnasium. The boom supports a shielded nuclear reactor for power generation.

Below: This design for a 400-man commercial space station was proposed for the 1990's. The tubular central area contains power, storage, recreation and computer sections and a docking bay for visiting space shuttles. Each of two cylinders at far right are multi-story crew modules for 200 people; they revolve to provide artificial gravity. Other cylinders are industrial modules, as in the earlier design. The spade-like extension is a "space greenhouse" for growing food.

**Space station
(1990's concept)**

Projects How to make a telescope

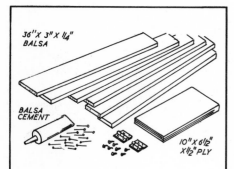

36" X 3" X 1⁄4" BALSA

BALSA CEMENT

10" X 6½" X ½" PLY

Materials To simplify construction the tubes are made from balsawood. Six sheets of 3" wide by ¼" thick balsa should be adequate. The mount is made from plywood and other readily obtainable materials. Work on the latter is made easier if an old camera tripod is available. The basic mount can be attached to this.

OBJECTIVE AND EYEPIECE LENSES

Lenses One long focus lens is required for the objective, and a short focus lens for the eyepiece. These should be good quality ground glass lenses (not plastic lenses) and can be obtained from firms specializing in the supply of optical accessories.

Edmund Scientific Co.,
300 Edscorp Building,
Barrington, N.J. 08007
Ehrenreich Photo-Optical Industries,
P.O. Box 519,
Garden City, N.Y. 11530
Spiratone,
135-06 Northern Boulevard,
Flushing, N.Y. 11354

The construction of an astronomical telescope can be extremely simple. It need consist only of an objective lens and an eyepiece lens, mounted at the opposite ends of two telescoping tubes. This type is known as a refracting telescope or refractor. More elaborate types of refractors may have groups of lens elements rather than single lenses, but the principle of working is the same. Refractors make good general purpose astronomical telescopes and are quite inexpensive to make.

The design of the telescope allows for the use of an objective lens up to 2¾ in. (70 mm.) diameter. It is recommended that you purchase a lens of near this size (2½ in. to 2¾ in.). A smaller lens can be used, but for best results do not choose one smaller than 2 in. (50 mm.) diameter. The focal length of this lens should be between 30 in. and 40 in. (750 mm. and 1,000 mm.).

The eyepiece lens can be much smaller in diameter. The actual size is not important provided its diameter is less than 2 in. (50 mm.) and its focal length is between 1 in. and 3 in. (25 mm. and 75 mm.).

You need to know the focal length of each of the lenses used in order to work out suitable lengths for the telescope tubes. You can check the focal length of a lens quite easily by using the lens to focus the sun's rays to a point image on a piece of paper, as shown in the diagram. Adjust the position of the paper until the sun's image appears as a tiny bright spot, which will scorch and blacken the paper if held in this position (i.e. the lens is being used as a "burning glass"). Measure the distance between the lens and paper. This will be the focal length of the lens.

Check the focal length of both lenses in this way.

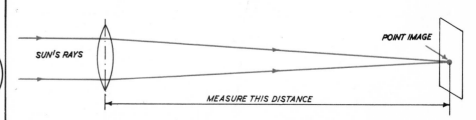

SUN'S RAYS

POINT IMAGE

MEASURE THIS DISTANCE

Magnification The magnification of your telescope can be worked out by dividing the focal length of the objective lens by the focal length of the eyepiece lens. For example, if the focal length of the objective lens is 30 in. (760 mm.) and the focal length of the eyepiece lens is 2 in. (50 mm.), the magnification of the telescope will be 30÷2=15 times (normally written 15×).

For best results, choose a combination of lenses which will give a magnification of between 10× and 15×. If you aim for higher magnification, the quality of the image will not be as good.

Dimensions for your telescope The length of the larger tube should be the same as the focal length of the objective lens. This need not be an exact dimension since the smaller tube slides in and out for adjustment of focus.

The length of the smaller tube can then be made 12 in. (300 mm.). This will provide several inches of adjustment with plenty of support for the inner tube. The telescope will be *in focus* when the position of the sliding tube is adjusted so that the distance between the objective lens and the eyepiece lens is equal to the sum of their focal lengths. Note that the objective lens is inset slightly for the front of its tube to act as a lens hood.

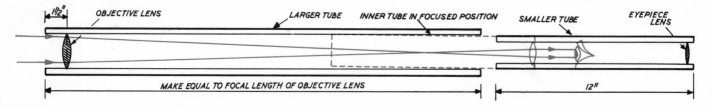

1½"   OBJECTIVE LENS   LARGER TUBE   INNER TUBE IN FOCUSED POSITION   SMALLER TUBE   EYEPIECE LENS

MAKE EQUAL TO FOCAL LENGTH OF OBJECTIVE LENS   12"

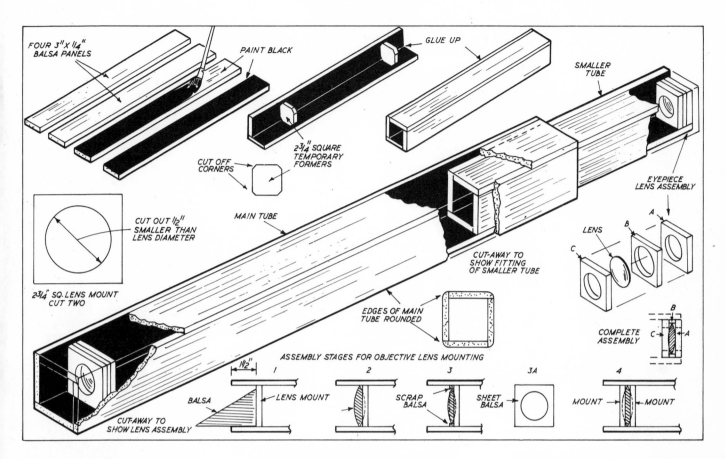

FOUR 3" X 1/4"
BALSA PANELS

PAINT BLACK

GLUE UP

SMALLER
TUBE

CUT OFF
CORNERS

2-3/4" SQUARE
TEMPORARY
FORMERS

EYEPIECE
LENS ASSEMBLY

CUT OUT 1/2"
SMALLER THAN
LENS DIAMETER

MAIN TUBE

LENS

A

B

C

2-3/4" SQ. LENS MOUNT
CUT TWO

CUT-AWAY TO
SHOW FITTING
OF SMALLER TUBE

COMPLETE
ASSEMBLY

EDGES OF MAIN
TUBE ROUNDED

C — A

ASSEMBLY STAGES FOR OBJECTIVE LENS MOUNTING

1/2"

1

2

3

3A

4

BALSA

LENS MOUNT

SCRAP
BALSA

SHEET
BALSA

MOUNT

MOUNT

CUT-AWAY TO
SHOW LENS ASSEMBLY

Constructing the telescope

The main plan now shows the construction of the telescope in detail. Having worked out a suitable length for the larger tube, cut four pieces of 3 in. × ¼ in. balsa to this length. One surface of each piece should then be painted with matte black paint (poster color is recommended, rather than ordinary paint). Allow to dry and if the surface of the balsa has roughened, sand down lightly to smooth.

Cut two 2¾ in. squares of ¼ in. sheet balsa to act as temporary formers and cut off the corners, as shown (this will prevent them sticking inside the tube). Glue two of the pieces of balsa together at right angles, as shown, using balsa cement, and place the temporary formers in position. Now glue on the other two pieces of balsa to complete the box which forms the main tube.

If necessary, use pins to hold the assembly together while the balsa cement is setting. The formers will hold the assembly "square". When the glue joints have set hard, these formers can be pushed out to give a completed, open tube.

The smaller tube is made in exactly the same way except that the size of each piece is 12 in. × 2¾ in; and the temporary formers to give "square" assembly are cut 2½ in. square. This tube must be a smooth sliding fit in the larger tube, so it is a good idea to *pin* the

four pieces together first to check for fit in the large tube. A tight fit is better than a very loose fit since this can always be relieved by sanding the tube down when finished.

Assembling the Objective Lens Cut two *lens mounts* from ¼" sheet balsa. These are 2¾" squares (to fit inside the large tube) each with a circular cutout about ½" smaller in diameter than the diameter of the lens. It will also be useful to cut a small *"set square"* from spare balsa sheet to assist in lining up the lens mounts.

Measure 1½ in. (about 40 mm.) in from one end of the tube and make a mark. Coat the edges of one mount with balsa cement and slide into position against this mark, using the balsa set square to make sure that it is exactly at right angles to the tube (stage 1 in the assembly diagram sequence).

Wait until the cement has set, then try the lens for position (stage 2). If the lens is slightly smaller in diameter than the tube, cut and fit pieces of scrap balsa to support it in position centrally and square, resting against the mount (stage 3). If the lens is considerably smaller in diameter than the tube, it will be easier to cut a separate mount to center the lens (stage 3A).

Once satisfied with the positioning of the lens, cement the second mount to hold it permanently in position (stage 4).

Assembling the Eyepiece Lens This is done in a similar manner except that the eyepiece lens is fitted on a level with one end of the smaller tube. Since the eyepiece lens will be considerably smaller in diameter than the tube, one mounting piece (B) is cut with a hole of the same diameter as the lens. Trim the thickness of this mount down as necessary so that when the other two lens mounts (A and C) are positioned to complete a "sandwich," these two mounts press firmly against each side of the lens to hold it secure. Get this right before attempting to cement the mounts into the tube.

Lining Up (Collimating) Immediately after cementing the eyepiece lens assembly into the end of the small tube, slide this tube into the larger tube and adjust to focus the telescope on some distant object. This will give you a chance to adjust the positioning of the eyepiece lens, if necessary, before the cement joint has set hard. If the two lenses are not lined up accurately, the eyepiece lens will not "see" the image formed by the objective lens.

If you have worked accurately, little or no lining-up should be necessary. On the other hand, if the objective lens is badly out of line, you may have to cut it free and reposition in order to get the telescope working properly.

Projects Mounting a telescope

MOUNTING THE TELESCOPE

A telescope cannot be held in the hand for moon or star viewing. It must be fitted to a mount to hold it steady, and at the same time permit the telescope to be swung or angled in the required direction. A square "collar" and a table are cut from ½ in. plywood to the dimensions shown. The collar is then fastened to the table with two metal hinges, as shown.

Two quadrant pieces are also required, which can be cut from ⅜ in. or ¼ in. plywood. Quadrant piece A has a curved slot cut out, as shown. This piece is then glued and screwed to one side of the collar, in line with the edge of the table.

Quadrant piece B is slightly deeper. It has a hole drilled in it in line with the curved slot of A. This second quadrant piece is glued and screwed to the edge of the table, lined up exactly with A.

The two quadrant pieces are then clamped together by a large-headed screw (preferably one with a milled head), two washers and a nut. Slacken off the nut and check that the collar will swing backwards easily—i.e., the curved slot in quadrant A slides over the screw. If not, trim the slot as necessary for easy movement.

The purpose of the two quadrant pieces should now be obvious. Slackening the nut (or screw head) frees the collar so that it can be tilted. Tightening the screw then locks the collar in the tilt position to which it has been set.

It now only remains to slide the telescope tube through the collar and glue the collar in place, but first mark the correct position for the collar on the telescope tube. This is found by closing the telescope (i.e., pushing the smaller tube in until only a short length protrudes), and then balancing the telescope on the fingers to find the point where it will be balance level. Mark this balance point. This is the position where the collar is glued in place.

Alternative Mountings The table can be mounted directly onto any sturdy camera tripod. A better idea is a permanent mount in some suitable part of the garden. A monopod is made from two lengths of metal tube, one being a sliding fit inside the other. The larger tube is set up vertically in a concrete base and needs to be either 5 ft. (for standing) or 3 ft. (for sitting) above ground.

The smaller tube has the ends plugged with wood. The table is screwed to one end, so that the whole assembly simply drops into the larger tube to set the telescope up. The telescope is just as easily removed by lifting out of the fixed tube. The telescope can be swung to either side easily, and height adjustment is provided in a series of 2-in. steps by drilled holes and a split pin. These, and other details, are shown in the mount plan.

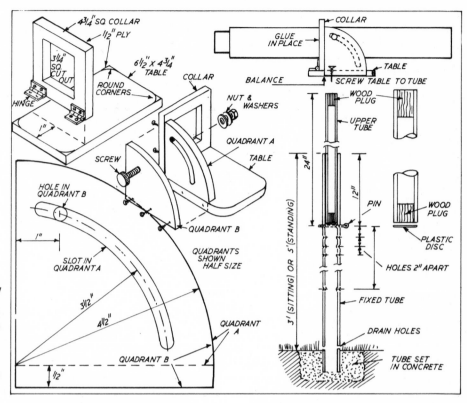

Limitation of Simple Lenses

Choosing the moon as a test subject for viewing, your telescope should give a clear, sharp image in the center of the field of view, becoming blurred and colored at the edges. This is because a simple lens breaks up white light and tends to "spread" it into rainbow colors, due to what is called *chromatic* aberration.

This can be cured to a large extent by reducing the effective diameter of the lens, or its *aperture*. Here is a useful field for experiment to improve your telescope.

Cut a number of squares of stiff cardboard to fit exactly inside the main tube (i.e. 2¾ in. square), with tags to make the masks easy to remove (see diagram below). Each of these masks has a different diameter circular cutout—1¾ in., 1½ in., 1¼ in., and so on. Try each in turn. The smaller the aperture diameter, the less the chromatic aberration, but at the same time the image will become increasingly darker.

Tips and Further Projects

Very few nights of the year are "perfect" for viewing. When conditions are not so good, and the image tends to drift in and out of focus, it can be worth experimenting with aperture masks again. Reducing the aperture should always improve the definition.

Another basic cause of poor definition is using too high a magnification. You can change the magnification of your telescope by changing the focal length of the eyepiece lens (i.e., use a higher focal length to reduce the magnification, and vice versa). You can make several smaller tubes, each fitted with an eyepiece lens of different focal length, and change from one to another to change the magnification of your telescope. The upper limit of magnification which you can hope to achieve and still get reasonable definition with a refracting telescope is about 30×.

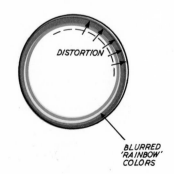

BLURRED 'RAINBOW' COLORS

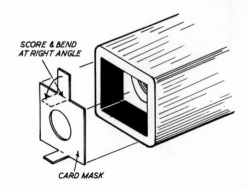

CARD MASK

Index

Illustration Credits

Key to the positions of illustrations: (T) top, (C) center,
(B) bottom and combinations; for example (TR) top right,
or (CL) center left.

Artists
Laurence Broderick/Garden Studio: 3(TL)
Burford Arts: 3(TR), 8(LC), 8–9(C)
David Jefferis: 17, 34–35(C), 42
Alexei Leonov: 18(TL) (CL)
Ken Osborn: 28-29(C) (BL) (BR)
John Smith: cover (TR), 11(C) (TR), 12(TL), 15, 22,
23(CL), 24(B), 25(T) (BL), 26(B), 28, 30, 31, 32, 33, 36,
37, 38, 39
Peter Taylor: 4(BC), 6(BR), 7(B), 12(BL)
Ron Warring: 44-46
John W. Wood and Associates: 6(L), 14(TL) (BL), 16,
18-19(C), 21, 23(TL) (TR) (BR), 27(TL), 35(BR)

Photographs and Prints
Bettmann Archive: 20(BL)
California Institute of Technology and Carnegie
Institution of Washington: cover (TL) (BL)

"Flight" Magazine: 12-13(C)
Jodrell Bank: cover (CL), 34(B)
Lockheed Solar Observatory: 10(CL) (BL)
Lund Observatory: 32-3(BC)
Mansell Collection: 4(TL) (B), 8(TL), 20(TL), 22(TL),
24(TL), 25(BC) (BR), 28(BL)
Philip Bono of McDonnell-Douglas Astronautics: 6–7(C),
27(TR) (C), 43(TR) (B)
MGM: 26(B)
Michael Holford: 10(TL)
Mitchell Beazley: 31(BR)
NASA: cover (C) (BR), 14(BR) (CL) (TL) (TR) (BL),
17(TR), 43(TL)
Novosti Press Agency: 5(TR) (BR), 12(BL), 13(CB),
17(BCL) (BL)
Radio Times Hulton Picture Library: 25(TR)
Ronan Picture Library: 3(CL), 20(TR), 35(TR)
Royal Astronomical Society: 11(TCL), 25(BCL) (TC),
29(BL) (TR)
Science Museum, London: 3(BL) (BR), 9(TL)
United States Information Service: 5(BL), 11(B),
13(BL) (BR), 29(TC), 35(CR) . .